Pursuit
Rise Of Mankind Book 5

John Walker

GW00374992

DISCLAIMER

This is a work of fiction. Names, characters, business, places, events, and incidents are either the products of the author's imagination or used in a fictitious manner. Any resemblance to actual persons, living or dead, or actual events is purely coincidental. This story contains explicit language and violence.

Blurb

Earth's mighty warship, *The Behemoth*, has been selected to receive the honor of formally joining the alliance. This momentous occasion opens new opportunities for the human race, a chance to help decide the fate of the universal government and participate in galactic affairs. As they prepare for the voyage and ceremony to come, not all are easy aboard the battleship.

Clea An'Tufal, liaison aboard *The Behemoth*, wakes from a revelatory dream. Her first assignment ended in tragedy, the ship she served on was destroyed in a massive battle. Just before the final shot forced them to evacuate, she discovered a signal, an enemy secret that could change the tide of the war.

Unfortunately, this information was stolen by a head wound, robbing her of all details regarding the mission. Now, it's come back to her and she believes the information may still be out there in the wreckage of her former berth. The trick is to convince not only her friend and Captain, Gray Atwell, of the importance of finding it but the council as well for if this is a mere obsession with a tragic event, the whole mission could be a dangerous waste of resources...or a revelation able to end the conflict once and for all.

Prologue

A blast struck the side of their vessel, causing it to shake violently. The hit felt so much worse than in the simulators and Clea An'Tufal wondered how they survived it. Surely anything capable of *moving* the entire ship had to have gotten through the shields. Horror stories from the more experienced officers came back to haunt her, of times when the enemy blasted a cruiser to dust in a single pass.

At least that didn't happen this time.

Clea focused on her work, trying to ignore the hammering of her heart and a rising sense of panic. This engagement, her first, seemed like a reasonable one. Eight alliance ships took on four of the enemy. Outnumbering their foes two to one sounded good in theory but analysis suggested their opponents actually thrived on encounters where they were outnumbered.

Her hands flew over her controls, scanning the enemy vessels for any sign of weakness, any advantage the kielans might take advantage of. They seemed like unstoppable titans, creatures intent on killing without remorse or chance for parlay. Most forgot how they first met and what started the war. It barely mattered since no one had spoken to one of the enemy since long before Clea was born.

The war itself didn't start for several years after contact had been broken. History books stated after cooperation became impossible, the kielans moved on and didn't look back. Whatever they said or did at the end pushed these zealots to an extreme of war. The attacks, merciless and sudden, began and continued on year after year.

Clea watched her screen for a moment as two alliance vessels flanked one enemy. They hammered it with pulse cannons, taking some licks but tearing through the shields. As the enemy hull cracked and split, a cheer resounded in her department. She checked her scan and sure enough, they finished one off.

Three to go.

Fighters screamed by, engaging in dogfights throughout the area. Their chatter cluttered up scans, filling the area with white noise which had to be filtered through. Clea wrote a program to do so when she was still in the academy and applied it at the start of the battle. Piercing through the interference, she focused on one ship which seemed to be staying out of the fight.

What're you doing back there?

Their power readings were maximum, they'd taken no damage and to her reckoning, hadn't fired a shot. They just sat there, waiting. *Maybe it's the command ship.* They knew little about the enemy and how they worked. Rank hierarchy and even specifics about their vessels remained mysterious. The latter came from the fact few of their ships were *exactly* the same.

Maybe their captains are allowed to personalize.

Most of the information the kielans had about the enemy came down to *maybes* and *theories*. Clea hadn't been in the service long enough to have as many as some of her fellow crew but she started to form a few. This fight alone gave her ample cause to start guessing. An opponent with no face might be easier to kill but it made it hard to know *why* they had to.

One of the kielan ships called out a mayday. Their shields went down and fighters hammered it from every direction. She checked just as their power core erupted, annihilating the small attackers around it. The suddenness of it meant no one escaped before it exploded. Every man and woman aboard had to be dead.

"I'm on survivors," someone shouted behind her.

Good, I don't want the duty of scanning for bodies.

Clea blinked hard, forcing herself to focus. She stared at her screen intently, trying to breach the interference of the enemy's drive core. Their shields fended off physical attacks but their engines emitted so much noise, they could only glean the most obvious details about their opponents.

One of those was an assumption about communication. They *believed* to know when they tried to send messages afar but that was based on pure energy casting away from the ship. They could even block it by causing enough interference themselves but there was no code to crack, not that they discovered.

Furthermore, they could detect their power reserves but even when they'd damaged one of their ships, they weren't suddenly granted a view of the internal values of the ships. They couldn't gather intel on ship layout or crew composition. Attempts at hailing them, more in the early days than recently, were always met with silence.

Many believed the enemy could hear them but refused to listen. Some suggested that was not the case, that they simply blocked all attempts at conversation because they had no intention of speaking to their victims. Many hoped to be able to force a conversation, to try appealing to any shred of conscience they may have.

Some of the rank and file soldiers couldn't be *totally* brainwashed. They had to have families and friends back home, the same as the kielans. Maybe internal revolt was possible if only they heard the desperate cries of the people they so mercilessly killed.

Another enemy vessel went up, this one by the combined efforts of fighters and one of the capital ships. They unleashed torrents of blaster fire in a concentrated section near the bridge. Clea checked the readings to see what she might learn from the assault. Her people pinpointed a specific area, no more than eighty meters around and battered it.

Excellent coordination.

"No survivors," someone called. A solemn cloud fell over their department. Clea sighed and continued her work on that lone vessel.

Wait a minute...what's this?

Clea noted a pattern to some energy emitting from the ship, something that *seemed* random merely because it took so long to repeat. One of her personal applications found the consistency and alerted her. She brought it up for further analysis, saving it to the ship's storage unit. It came from what might've been their bridge, connecting to the other ship.

Communications? Clea hummed, trying to work quicker. The computer program continued to diagram the pattern, offering suggestions to what it might be for along the way.

Remote control of the entire other ship.

A constant line of voice communications specially coded.

Transfer of energy to provide bolstered shields and weapons.

Then, the energy signal burst from the vessel as it had in the past, moving far off from the battle. Clea checked and grinned. The pattern was the same only mired in interference. *I found something!* The data got saved immediately and she started a deep dive analysis to determine exactly what it was used for.

Another blow to the ship caused such a violent tremor, Clea was tossed to the floor. Others in her department cried out as some maintained their seats and others collapsed. She pushed herself to her feet just as the alarm went off. Red lights overhead began flashing. A voice piped through the speakers.

"Alert, alert. All hands evacuate. Repeat, all hands evacuate. Hull breach on deck seven through thirteen."

Oh no, Clea thought, *the engines are on deck ten!*

She climbed to her feet and went back to her station, tapping at the screen to download the data. Someone grabbed her by the arm. "We have to go! Now!" Clea tried to shake them off but they wouldn't let go. "That's an *order* Zanthari! Move it!"

Clea cursed under her breath as something exploded behind her sending sparks flying into the air. She rushed out of the room with the others, hustling down a hallway as hoses burst and the entire ship shook. When she sat at her terminal working, she could fight the fear but now, in a blind run to the escape pods, full panic grabbed her stomach.

They rounded a corner, two hundred meters from their destination when something hit them again. *We're already done, you monsters! Why are you still shooting us?* Another heavy shake sent her against the wall, her head bouncing off the metal panel. Queasiness overtook her and she couldn't feel her limbs.

I think I'm dying…

As she fell in slow motion, someone caught her, dragging her backward. The ceiling became dark then red, dark and red over and over before consciousness slipped away. The last sound she heard came from the automated emergency system. "Alert, alert. All hands evacuate. Repeat, all hands evacuate."

Chapter 1

Clea woke with a start, her heart racing in her chest. The dream remained fresh in her mind, gnawing at her as she climbed out of bed and moved over to her desk. Tapping the computer screen, it came to life and she began to write down the events so she wouldn't forget them.

How did I forget all about that event? Indeed, she'd been in several battles but that one in particular totally escaped her. Perhaps the injury, she did remember being hurt for several days but somehow glossed over how it happened. *Maybe I didn't want to remember. If it was as bad as the dream, then I understand. I never wake up scared.*

A voice echoed through the halls of the Behemoth, Ensign Agatha White telling everyone they would make Earth orbit in three hours. Clea's alarm would've woken her in an hour. She wanted to be on the bridge when they made orbit, to see them safely returned to where they belonged. They had a great deal to report, from the mining operation mission to first contact with a bristly new culture to a dramatic space battle.

At least repairs didn't take long. Before they left, they needed to perform some minor repairs but finished before jumping. Once they were prepared to go home, everyone remained on duty through the process. Not a single member of the crew wanted to be surprised by a second mishap though Clea was certain nothing would happen.

Maury Higgins remained in the medical bay recovering from being shot. The doctors said he would come out okay but it would take time. When they arrived back at Earth, he would be transferred to another medical facility where he could mend properly. He already made it clear he wanted to come back immediately.

"You'd have to amputate everything to keep me away."

Clea found the image disturbing but the sentiment seemed good natured.

They were close enough to the alliance ships for her to access historical records. She brought up a log of the battle in a mineral rich sector some distance from their home world. Four enemy ships against eight alliance vessels, that's what the log titled it. *Not very compelling but descriptive I suppose.*

The overall result of the conflict was three kielan vessels were destroyed and four of the enemy. Hers, the *Tempered Steel*, was the second of their ships to be taken out. Various people wrote logs about the affair, explaining the tactics used, analyzing the failures and successes of the mission.

Clea frowned, trying to find her own log but couldn't locate one. She did locate a roster of individuals who were injured or slain. Her name appeared on the list, near the bottom as *crew transferred to medical*. This required a cross reference check for more information. Her eyes widened when she found her file.

How did I forget being in the hospital for six days?

Clea remembered it being bad but six days seemed excessive. The report stated she was unconscious for the first three days. Afterward, she recovered quickly and moved on to the psychiatrists. There, she endured a number of conversations about her post battle state of mind. She recalled not being too badly off, especially since she could not remember the destruction of her ship.

Small blessing back then but why remember now? They warned her the memories might come back at any time. She didn't think they would through a dream. She never gave much stock to the ramblings of night time fantasies but this felt entirely too vivid to be a flight of fancy. This held information she could not believe she lost.

What information did I find? And how much of what I just witnessed was made up? My mind may have filled in the blanks with something more interesting than the truth.

Clea made a request for more information, sending it to the tech officer aboard the kielan ship. Storage capacity was never a problem so they would have access to the documents, even from all the way back then. She hoped to find more information than the cursory glance into the public documents. Her new rank might even afford her some priority to get her request finished.

One can only hope but I doubt I'll find anything particularly exciting in what they send. I'm afraid my personal information is probably lost.

Clea read back over what she wrote and felt thankful she'd done so. The dream already faded from her mind, disappearing into the ether. She decided to shrug it off for the time being and went to clean up. They had a full docket when they arrived at Earth and she wanted to be fresh for the interrogation like briefings she expected, both from the humans and her own kind.

Everyone wants a story and considering how many we have, I'm guessing this'll take a while.

***

Tim Collins and Amos Roper were set to be transferred from the ship to military authorities the moment the Behemoth made Earth orbit. Military guard prepared a highly secure shuttle which was destined for a maximum security facility. There, the two men would wait for their trial, which surely would not go their way.

Captain Gray Atwell met with Commander Adam Everly and Lieutenant Colonel Marshall as soon as they made Earth space to discuss everything that happened. They penned an extensive report regarding their investigation and detailed the actions of the three traitors. Lieutenant Theresa Conway's final moments of violence were also documented, right up to her death while holding a hostage.

When they were done, Gray insisted on speaking with Tim. Adam advised against it. "What good will come from it, sir? He's going down for what he did. There's nothing he can say that would make any difference now, don't you think?"

"I trusted that man," Gray replied. "I considered him a fine officer and he betrayed *all* our trust. I'll look him in the eye before I turn him over, while he's still under my command, and see if I can tell why he did it."

"Because he had sex," Marshall replied. "Conway turned him but it wasn't hard because she used Jameson against him. She developed an asset with her body and there wasn't a whole lot he could do about it. Smart as Collins was, he had enough naivety to be taken in by a pretty face...and a forceful one too from my analysis."

"So you're saying he betrayed us all over a chance with a woman?" Gray shook his head. "I don't buy it. He had to know they weren't going to succeed. His life would be over. And what if their tampering killed us all? I need to see him myself now that things are calmed down."

Adam nodded. "Yes, sir. Just...don't be too disappointed with the lack of answers you're going to receive. I don't think he's going to have a good explanation."

"He can at least try."

Gray went to the brig alone and let the guards know he wanted to speak with Collins but to leave the man in his cell. They escorted him back and he dismissed them, standing straight with his hands clasped behind his back. Collins reclined on the bed, staring up at the ceiling. He didn't look anything like himself, drained and pale. Nothing like the vibrant officer who had served on the bridge since before they finished the ship.

"Now's your chance to talk," Gray said. "If you've got anything to say to me personally."

"I don't think so, sir." Collins replied. He spoke in monotone, barely moving as he did so.

"Don't say anything!" Roper shouted. "They'll just use it against us!"

"Guards," Gray spoke calmly but he struggled to contain a surge of anger. "Remove Ensign Roper to Interrogation Room Two."

The guards complied and Roper did not act as placid as his co-conspirator. Even though he'd been shot in the leg, he still struggled, shouting at Collins to keep his mouth shut. Gray waited for him to be out of earshot before returning his full attention to the cell. He drew a deep breath and tried again.

"I think you've got plenty to say and I expect to hear something. I trusted you, Tim. You were one of my finest officers. Even after the event, you stepped up and headed to astrogation. Was that you feeling some guilt over what you'd done? I want answers. How could you betray us all?"

"Sir…" Tim finally sat up, but stared at the floor now instead of the ceiling. "I…Conway brought me the orders from Jameson and showed them to me. She knew I'd worked with him and made it clear he expected my cooperation. I…tried to tell them they were insane but they didn't want any kind of warnings. They wanted results."

"So you just went along with it?" Gray scowled. "Without any more pushback?"

"At one point, Conway threatened to take the orders to her CO and say they were found in my quarters. She was with security after all. There...were other things too..."

"Such as?"

Tim sighed, rubbing his eyes. "I'd never been with someone before..."

Gray knew his meaning and decided not to push. "So she...helped with that?"

Tim nodded.

"I see. So it took Jameson, threats and sex to push you over the edge? Let me ask you this. Why didn't you come to me or Adam? Why not tell us immediately about the plot?"

"Roper talked about snitches and what happened to them on space ships." Tim blinked several times. "I shouldn't have listened but it all sounded so reasonable back then. Now, after the fact, I don't know why I went along. I can think of a thousand things to have done differently but they don't matter now. I've already gone down the rabbit hole and there's no turning back."

"You're right." Gray turned away. "You're quite right. I'm sorry it came to this, Tim. I hope you realize they'll throw the book at you for what you've done. With Conway out of the way, they'll hang as much as they can on the shoulders of you and Roper. If you don't get executed, you can look forward to a lifetime sentence on a mining facility."

"I know, sir." Tim stood up. "May I personally apologize for betraying your trust in particular?"

Gray looked over his shoulder, considering the man for several long moments. He didn't feel entirely charitable toward the former lieutenant nor did he lean toward offering him any comfort. He deserved to wallow in his guilt and think about what he'd done. Too many lives were risked for their idiotic agenda.

"I do *not* accept it. You broke your oath on your own and you can pay for it, without forgiveness from anyone." Gray left him there as he slumped back on the bed, certainly a broken man.

Adam was right. I probably shouldn't have bothered.

***

Gray presented his findings concerning the new culture of the Emancipated and Founders, sending a full report to the council. They worked together with the kielans to get a diplomatic vessel sent out there right away, someone to help them prepare for the coming war. Much as Earth had when they encountered the enemy.

Considering the combat effectiveness of their potential allies, hopes were high that they might contribute greatly to the war effort. The Earth council exhibited hope on the subject as did the kielans who were brought in immediately. If their shield technology worked so well without enhancement, bolstering them would prove a great benefit.

Clea and Lieutenant Oliver Darnell were tasked with presenting their findings about the culture as well, sending their complete technical observations. Each of them were quite complimentary, especially concerning their communication protocols and security. It was primitive by comparison but they felt some of the techniques would benefit the alliance as well.

Cultural data was transferred over, everything about the history the Behemoth collected. This data gave a good idea of where they were coming from and some of the diplomatic challenges their people had to worry about. Ultimately, they would be approached with caution but the kielans had become quite good at indoctrinating new cultures.

***

Tim and Amos presented their evidence to the Criminal Investigation Division in the company of legal representation. They made a deal to testify against Admiral Jameson in exchange for life sentences. The whole process took less than a day for them to talk and sign the paperwork. Gray, Adam, Marshall and Major Harrington Bean, who interrogated the men, provided a recorded testimony under the supervision of the lead prosecutor.

They checked the Admiral's office, looking at every in and out message around the noted time frame. Several gaps were detected, intentionally deleted by a technician. This young man was questioned hard and gave up his part of the conspiracy as well. What helped even more was that he worried about his actions and kept a copy of some of the messages.

This damning evidence helped them proceed up the pole. The orders sent to the Behemoth came from Jameson's personal assistant, Major Alister Trace. He was arrested at his home and questioned. He tried to take the blame fully on himself but a search of his own schedule and computer archives suggested collusion with the admiral. After another full day of grilling, he finally folded.

The man had a family and they brought up how miserable a lengthy trial would be for them. He didn't want to be responsible for causing undo stress to those in his own household, so his loyalty for the admiral took second place to that of his wife and children. Once they had his testimony bagged, the CID was ready to move.

They presented the data privately to Chief of Military Operations, Daniel Burke. It took nearly four hours to go through everything and in the end, it was decided to bring the admiral in and confront him with his crimes. The conversation took less than an hour before he admitted to wrong doings but would not name specifics.

Often, high ranking military men such as Jameson would've been allowed to simply resign and retire. The nature of his particular crime made Daniel loath to leave the man his total freedom. There was another factor to consider as well. An anti-alliance faction had grown amongst the people of Earth and he represented their leader.

Ultimately, they did allow him the dignity of surrendering his position but insisted he live where he was told under guard for the rest of his life. He did not have a family and considering the alternative, being dragged through the court and having his entire legacy besmirched, he accepted the deal.

Daniel elected to have him moved to a military facility in Alaska where none of the protests took place nor did anyone particularly seem to care about what happened in space. They closed the case with Tim and Roper being transported off planet to work on a mining vessel elsewhere in the system.

Gray met with Daniel later to receive a briefing. The divisive factions on Earth were being dealt with through covert channels as the intelligence community stepped in to help break up their structure by removing leaders to their causes. Ultimately, they represented a small percentage of people however, they had loud voices and demanded they be heard.

"This is none of your concern," Daniel said. "We have another mission for you coming up soon."

"I hope we can have a little downtime before we head back out," Gray replied. "My people are hoping to get some rest and we need a couple of experts to help us with essential repairs."

"Yes, we fully intend for you to have the next week and a half free. Make sure your people get leave time and coordinate with the kielans on the maintenance." Daniel grinned. "Besides, I wouldn't send you away before we Christen our new vessel. I'm told they'll be ready to fire up the pulse engine in the next few days."

"That's great news," Gray replied. "Have you picked out a crew for her yet?"

"The volunteers lined up, especially after news of your exploits out there. Every adventurous young person you can imagine from the academy and other branches have come forward and want a chance to go into space. If you want to rotate any folks out, we're looking for training opportunities."

"Send me a list and we'll take a look. I'm sure we can accommodate some of that and help get people the expertise needed for their positions." Gray took a deep breath. "So what's the mission?"

"We'll be sending you to the kielan home world as an ambassador this time. Much like Mei'Gora, we'd like you to address their council and accept Earth's full membership into the alliance."

"That's a big honor," Gray said. "I'm surprised you don't want to come with us...take it yourself."

"There are a few reasons you were picked," Daniel replied. "One, they requested you. After helping with the research facility *and* the mine, you've proven yourself to them. Two, you've earned it after all you've been through. It would be nice to have an easier assignment for a change."

Gray held up a hand to interrupt him. "Don't forget, that's what you said about the research facility."

Daniel smirked. "Yes, I know. Anyway, this is their *home* world. I can't imagine anything's going to happen there. So three, and this one can come off sounding raw, the council decided sending any of us might not be safe."

"Which contradicts two." Gray smiled to offset the comment. "I understand the meaning. But you're right, it makes us sound expendable."

"You know you're not but...well...this is a desperate time for the war effort. You'll be accompanied back by one of the kielan vessels and the other will remain. We're well on the way to a third ship and they're going to help us with that too. I think they're cooperation has been stellar. I'm hoping we can prove that to the dissidents that say we should sever ties."

"Accepting membership with the alliance should help a little," Gray replied. "Either that, or they'll rebel harder. They might feel like they have no recourse but to take up arms."

"Leave that to the intelligence teams," Daniel replied. "You worry about heading back to their home, getting us on their list and getting home safely."

"I'll plan the mission and take some time off myself," Gray said. "I definitely feel like I need some time on the ground."

"Good idea, Captain." Daniel stood and Gray followed suit, shaking the man's hand. "Thank you for all you've done, Captain. I'll be writing commendations for all of your senior officers. Catch up with me before you're ready to depart and we'll speak again."

"Of course, sir. Thank you for your time."

Gray left and established communication with Adam Everly. The commander answered a moment later. "How'd it go?"

"Good," Gray replied. "We've got another mission but we don't leave for a week and a half. Make sure we get a leave schedule going and give people as much down time as possible. Tech crews from the kielan ship will be helping with the maintenance."

"What's the mission?"

"Diplomacy," Gray said. "We're going to the kielan home world to accept full membership into the alliance."

"That's great news. Maybe we'll be able to take the fight to the enemy soon."

"Perhaps. Anyway, get that roster going. I'm going to plan the mission, check the resupply schedule and get some time off myself."

"Well earned, sir. I'll see you soon."

Gray took a moment to soak in the Florida weather, drawing a deep breath of fresh air. He'd been shipboard for so long, standing on solid ground felt odd. He intended to take as much time as he could *outside* during his time off. Maybe a camping trip…anything without technology or starships.

I need some distance to bounce back. This week will be fantastic. Then, back at it.

Chapter 2

Clea took up residence in a hotel near the military base. Civilian amenities beat the military accommodations and after the month she had, she wanted to enjoy some comfort. Once they made planet side, Gray disappeared into the bureaucratic side of the armed force so she figured she wouldn't see him for a few days.

She anticipated some trouble trying to get the room but the front desk person didn't even look at her twice. Once she got into her room, she checked the internet for images of humans to see if any came with her hair color. Apparently, many of them used dye to alter their appearance and some even wore contacts to change that as well.

Vanity? Or just a desire to stick out? Florida in particular had quite a few people who visited high end salons to get a unique look. *They'll love the rest of my people then. We come in all variety of colors.*

The thought came as ironic considering the group of humans demanding distance from the alliance. Kielans tended to be the easiest going species in the galaxy when it came to other cultures. They helped dozens reach their potential. Several of those groups also treated them with suspicion but few actively suggested they should be ostracized.

After all we've done for the humans, too. What a shame.

Clea ate a decent meal and watched a couple of films before preparing to sleep. The bed, a king size affair, made her accommodations on the ship look like a plank. Crawling in, she immediately relaxed. The soft sheets and extra pillows provided a luxury she had not known since before leaving home for the military.

Even on downtime during the refit of the Behemoth, she stayed in Spartan apartments on base. This extravagance felt one hundred percent worth every coin she had to spend.

Her mind drifted until sleep took her, bringing her to a deep state of unconsciousness. She found herself startling awake, sitting in her quarters on board the *Tempered Steel*. The alarm ticked nearby and she shut it off, checking to see she had thirty minutes to report to her post.

Throwing herself through a quick refresh, she donned her uniform and rushed down the hall to the tech lab. In her haste, she bumped into a fellow Zanthari, one she attended school with. His name was Megs Di'Weran, an engineer.

"Late for post again?" Megs asked.

"Not really," Clea called back. "But almost! Want to meet for dinner at the end of shift?"

"Yeah, sounds good! See ya!"

Clea grinned, finding ease in her assignment and wondering about the strange memory prior to waking up. Was it a dream? Going to bed in that foreign world...living amongst another race? It didn't seem possible and as she hustled into the tech lab, she felt far more at home than she had only an hour earlier.

What an absolutely bizarre dream! I should probably talk to the ship's councilor about it. There must be a reason behind it.

"Welcome to the land of the living, Miss An'Tufal." The voice came from her commanding officer, Vinthari Tri'Casa. "Sleep well?"

"Yes, sir." Clea sat down. "I'm not late though, sir…"

"That's why I'm giving you a hard time." The others around her chuckled. "This must be a first."

"Sorry to impress?" Clea gave him a sheepish look. "I had quite the dream."

"I'm sure we don't need to hear about it, Zanthari." Tri'Casa gestured to her console. "Get to work before you come up with any other stories for us to hear."

He went about his business and she logged in, peering over the current work load. Most of her day was spent fixing computer problems throughout the ship and chasing down readings externally when that work dried up. The others around her had various specific duties but they could bounce ideas off one another.

Clea liked the team. They were solid performers one and all. Some of them she attended school with as well and, like her, this was their first assignment. The nearest person to her leaned close, a woman her age named Reya Mal'Doren. She looked back at the Vinthari before speaking.

"Why are you really on time?" Reya asked.

"Because my alarm woke me up for a change," Clea replied. "I wasn't up as late as normal."

"No after shift programming?"

"Nope. What about you? Were you slumming for fellas in the mess again?"

Reya blushed. "Come on, Clea! That's not funny."

"Hey, I wasn't trying to be. More power to you if you find a guy on board."

"You telling me no one's struck your fancy?" Reya scowled. "What about Megs?"

"Ew." Clea shook her head. "He's like my brother. We were in the academy together *and* the same secondary. I've known him forever."

"Some of those can turn into more."

"Not for me. I'm career." Clea shrugged. "I've got to find something to set me apart, you know? Everyone in my family's done amazing things. My sister's at one of the research outposts."

"Oh! Which one?" Reya's eyes widened.

"I don't know. A secret one I guess. She couldn't tell us."

"Wow…no wonder you're working after hours so much."

"See? I've got huge shoes to fill. Both my parents are big names and I'm just a technical person."

"Hey, you're a genius with code though." Reya patted her shoulder. "Don't forget that."

"Yeah, thanks." Clea shook her head. "I hope it's enough."

A voice behind them interrupted their conversation. "I just got a ping from the bridge. It seems we're moving in to engage a number of enemy vessels."

"Engage?" Reya sat up straight. "As in...we're about to get into a fight?"

"Focus on your terminal, Reya," Vinthari Tri'Casa said. "Let's do this by the numbers, folks. Our data can turn the tide of a battle. Only essential incidents should be focused on. Everyone put your attention toward scans and assistance. I expect to get some good data out of this fight so let's keep our minds on the prize."

Clea turned her attention to her computer and started running through her program list. The world felt strange, the situation surreal. She'd been here before, a sense of deja vu hit her but where had some come up with the term? Gray told her...but...that would mean this whole situation...

The ship shook from an attack and she jumped, sitting up straight in the hotel room bed covered in sweat. *That was vivid! What is going on?* She got up and went into the bathroom, turning on the hot water for a shower. As the room began to steam, she peered into the mirror, watching her reflection vanish in the fog.

I need to talk to someone about this. But who? Gray? The doctor? One of them might be able to help but then again, we're all busy with our downtime. They may be off with family. I can probably deal with this alone...or maybe I should speak to Mei'Gora. He's still here and might even have a better understanding. Maybe he remembers the fight.

Clea sent Anthar Mei'Gora a request for a meeting in the next few days before cleaning up. When she returned to bed, she hoped to make it through the rest of the night without another dream. She'd had enough of revisiting the past through sleep. Especially considering how intense it seemed to be.

I miss Reya and Megs. I wonder how they're doing. I know they both made it out of there…they sent me congratulations when I took on the liaison assignment. Reya's in particular stuck out. One line in particular remained in Clea's mind: 'you'll finally stand on your own in the family. Congratulations! You deserve this more than most! Good luck!'

That was the last time the two communicated and it had been too long. She made a mental note to write her in the morning and inquire after how her life had been treating her. Maybe they could get together when Clea returned home. But for the moment, she wanted to enjoy the rest of the night in that fabulous bed.

There may not be many luxurious nights in her future. She had to make the ones she was given count.

***

The crew of the Behemoth took their downtime gratefully. Meagan Pointer spent the first day with Rudy, traveling with him to present the sad news about his lost pilot. They drank together and parted ways the next morning, each heading to spend the rest of their time with family members.

Hoffner spent his time at the academy, relaxing with an old mentor who retired to teach. They kept it low key, quiet evenings watching videos, drinking and relating war stories. The Behemoth's missions made for some great ones. Some of them might even end up in the infantry books for training purposes.

Maury spent his time in the hospital recovering. Though his prognosis was positive, he was not likely to make the next mission. This really set him off but considering where he'd been shot, he was lucky to be alive. Any protests fell by the wayside when he received that little reminder.

Oliver and Paul spent time together playing games off base at the former's parents' house. Redding, Adam and Agatha all visited their respective families. Many

Gray went camping, using a cabin that his father bought when he was young. He kept his activities low key, fishing and hiking in the days and relaxing by the fireplace at night. The silence appealed to him but at the same time, it felt unnerving for the first few days. By the time he got used to it, he wondered how he'd feel when he returned to the constant hum of the ship.

All of them took their peace where they could find it, knowing full well it might be their last for a while. Each of them, in their way, knew they stood at a turning point in human history. Not because of their next mission but their discovery of new intelligent beings, visiting solar systems on the other side of the galaxy and the war with an enemy that wanted to destroy every other being in the universe.

The pressure was great but they'd proven up to the challenge so far. As they made their way back to active duty, none of them felt regret at going back to work. Excitement filled the shuttles heading back up top side and as they settled back into the familiar quarters and duties of ship life, they looked forward to what fate might have in store for them next.

***

Clea's meeting with Mei'Gora got cancelled by one of his assistants. He sent his regrets and suggested they get together a few days after her leave ended. She replied with a polite thank you, but declined to reschedule. She had a feeling they'd be gone before he found the time.

Instead, she busied herself with visiting engineering. Several technicians worked with the kielan engineers to make modifications and repairs, resulting in a fully functional jump drive. She read through their changes and felt confident that any tampering would be *much* more difficult. All around, they did great work.

Commander Janet Weatherby took over as Chief Engineer in Maury's absence. As his second, she was one of the only people he personally trusted. Clea had worked with her several times and also felt good about the choice.

Security also increased around the technical areas, with armed guards standing by as check points for anyone wanting to visit the engine room. The technicians grumbled about it but not too loudly. After what happened to Tim and Amos, everyone understood the need for heightened failsafes.

Clea saw she had a briefing just after lunch with the other senior officers. Gray mentioned they would be starting their next mission, departing Earth for a safe jump position before the end of third shift. She wondered what might be in store when a second meeting popped up for her to talk to Gray in private.

I wonder if that's good or bad. I suppose I'll find out.

Gray kept the group meeting quick and to the point. Command was sending the Behemoth to the Kielan home world where they would formally accept admittance to the alliance. Clea's heart leaped in her chest. *I'm going home!* It had been several years since she visited and the thought of returning now thrilled her.

Then, some reality kicked in. *I have to face my parents after what happened to my sister.*

They already knew what happened and had written her back to tell her how sorry they were she had to endure the situation. Now they'd get the chance to lament together. It wouldn't all be negative but what a sour way to return from a long tour. *We'll make the best of it somehow. There's still a lot of good to talk about.*

"I hope you all had a fantastic leave," Gray said. "We'll be breaking orbit in the next two hours so check in with your departments and get ready to go. Dismissed."

Clea waited for the others to leave and closed the door, returning to her seat. Gray grinned. "How was your time off?"

"It was good," Clea replied. "I just rested. Tried to see Mei'Gora but he was too busy."

"Ah, anything urgent?"

"Personal and professional but not urgent."

"I wanted to talk to you about visiting your home," Gray said. "First off, I hope you're excited."

"I am. It's been a long time since I've been there."

Gray nodded. "Good. Second, I'm hoping we'll have some time for you to show me around the way I showed you Earth. I don't want to take time way from your family, of course...but I'm anticipating we'll be there for a little while."

"Yes, likely. There're ceremonies to perform of course. We'll be expected to follow them. Your people are to be welcomed into the fold, so to speak. That'll be good for everyone. Earth will have a say in galactic politics. I suppose right there, that's what the council has always wanted, right?"

"Probably. A chance to help decide our own fate. One thing we're particularly good at is being busy bodies too. We like to help, even when it's not wanted."

"I saw that with the new culture we encountered. You refused to leave them to die even after they attacked us."

Gray shrugged. "I won't leave helpless victims to those monsters. I've seen what they can and will do."

"We both have." Clea thought back to her dream and felt a film of sweat form on the back of her neck. "I think you'll find my home to your liking. At least the capital. The weather is just as extreme as Earth...that is, the regions offer the full spectrum of temperatures. At the very least, I'll take you to the zoo. You'll certainly appreciate that."

"I can't think of a better way to see your culture." Gray stood up. "We should get to the bridge. I just wanted a quick chat with you. I hadn't seen you since we left."

"Did you go camping?"

"I did...and it was as soothing as I'd hoped."

"Ready for something to go wrong?"

Gray chuckled. "You're reading my mind."

"Or isn't the saying...like minds?"

"Great minds think alike."

"There you go."

"After you, Clea."

"I'm glad to be back sir."

Chapter 3

Clea received the logs she requested about the battle while she sat on the bridge. They'd started traveling to their jump point and been away from Earth's orbit for over an hour. She brought up the information and started reading, unable to fend off some hope that she might find something new.

Unfortunately, the parts she was most interested in, her saved files, were not there. They'd been lost with the ship supposedly. Other logs survived, indicating where the battle took place. Salvage teams deemed the area too dangerous to risk collecting left behind technology. Many fights meant the area was dominated by considerable debris and apparently, there was already a large asteroid field nearby.

Any essential equipment was deemed destroyed. Whatever's left will not matter to the alliance.

Clea didn't feel as certain. A good salvage team would find something out there. In fact, she figured unsanctioned ships probably visited the area and took things all the time. Whatever was out there probably got stripped down a long time ago. However, if those people didn't know what a storage drive looked like, it may have been overlooked.

Which would mean it could still be out there.

The *Tempered Steel* did not actually explode. It was split down the middle and depressurized. Much of it probably remained intact. *Why not visit the ship and see what happened?* She wished she received the information in person so she could ask just that question. Surely, some bureaucrat made the call after looking at the expense for an expedition.

"Captain?" Clea turned away from her data. "Can we speak for a moment in the ready room?"

"Absolutely." Gray stood up. "Adam, the bridge is yours."

"Yes, sir," Adam replied without looking up from his terminal.

Clea and Gray made their way into the small office just off the bridge and had a seat. "What's on your mind?" Gray asked.

"It may be nothing," Clea began, "but if we can get authorization, I think it'll be worth a look. On my first berth, we engaged four enemy vessels. My ship was destroyed or at least, rendered uninhabitable. We had to evacuate."

"Tough for your first time out," Gray said. "I know how you feel."

Clea frowned. "Yes, I know. I don't mean to bring up poor memories but this may have a silver lining. At the time of the attack, I was working on something…I believe I made a discovery, one which might help us a great deal."

"Do tell."

"I was analyzing the enemy throughout the engagement, looking for anything to help our ships get through their shields faster and cause more damage. In the process...I...I *think* I came up with a coded signal. Or something." Clea shook her head. "I can only barely remember."

"There's a story there," Gray pointed out. "Why are you just thinking of this now?"

Clea looked down, scowling. "I'm not sure. I...I dreamt about the battle. You see, I took a head injury while we abandoned ship and ended up in the hospital for six days. The psychologist told me I might recover my memories but I hadn't in years so I guess I just shrugged it off. Now, it's coming back to me and it feels like we might finding something there."

"Your teams didn't salvage the ship?"

"No, it's dangerous. The area has a lot of natural debris and of course, multiple ships worth of hazards as well." Clea shrugged. "Our people felt it wasn't practical to go in there but I'm of the opinion we should try. Again, if we get authorization, a quick investigation may turn something up and if not, we wouldn't have wasted too much time."

Gray nodded, looking thoughtful. "So we have to hop out to this area you're talking about, perform some salvage to see if you find anything and if you do, we can determine how it helps the war effort, is that it?"

"In a nutshell, sir…yes."

"Must've been some find if it's got you thinking about it."

Clea sighed. "I'm sure I should've remembered years ago. Back then, I might've just been lucky because I've done that job since then and never found anything I'd call a game changer. This feels big. Believe me, I wouldn't waste your time if I didn't think it absolutely necessary. Besides, we've proven to be pretty lucky so far, right?"

"Good and bad in equal measures I'm afraid," Gray replied. He smiled as he stood. "I'll go back to my office and contact the council before we make the jump. Thanks for bringing this to me."

"Don't thank me until we've found something," Clea said. "If I'm just crazy or it was all a hopeful dream, then I'll feel like a real ass."

"Sometimes hunches lead to great discoveries. Don't worry about it. We'll see what we can do, Clea. I just have to find a way to explain this that doesn't involve dreams. I'll talk to you soon."

"Thank you, sir." Clea returned to her post on the bridge and directed her attention to the various technical reports throughout the ship. She made her case and it was time to stop fixating on the past. Not that she could easily do so. A sense of urgency clung to her heart, one that made it feel as if she'd discovered one of the most important things of her career.

Again. Though it's probably not even there anymore. It's been far too long. I'm leading us on a fool's errand...but it could be so lucrative if I'm somehow right. Okay, there's a problem with the network links on deck seven. Not exactly my job, but I can focus on that. Here and now, Clea. That's the important thing for the time being. Remain focused.

***

Gray considered Clea's proposal as he headed for his office. She definitely wouldn't have brought it to him if she didn't think it was important but he felt rational enough to question the situation. Memories *could* come back to a person through dreams and that's why he was willing to make the request. If she was right and something important was hiding out there, they'd be fools to leave it.

And what's it really going to do to our schedule? We'll be done with the ceremony and ready to go home soon enough. A quick side trip won't hurt anything.

To sell the council, that was the important part of the equation. He believed he could do it but needed to think specifically how he would. *Maybe she discovered something in some logs that led her to believe we might want to look at the salvage again. The danger of it meant we should send a ship like the Behemoth.*

That was definitely one good story. *What else can I try?*

Ultimately, he wanted to avoid surfaced memories and work toward something more tangible. Command allowed them considerable latitude lately but this would be pushing it. If she found something in logs, then they'd likely want to see the records. Perhaps a little honest mixed with some omission would work best.

Gray sat behind his desk and fired up the long distance communication network. They were still within the solar system so lag would be almost nonexistent. As he waited for Daniel to pick up, he wondered what time it might be back home near the base. When Daniel's image appeared bleary eyed, illuminated by the screen, he figured it out.

"Gray," Daniel sounded surprised. "I didn't expect to hear from you soon. I hope this isn't terrible news. Not another attack?"

"No, sir," Gray replied. "I wanted to bring something to your attention and receive permission to append an objective to our mission. It should be little more than a minor detour but considering what it is, we'll need permission."

"What's going on?"

"Clea shared with me a major battle from their past, one which ended with four enemy ships being destroyed and three alliance vessels meeting the same fate. The sector was incredibly dangerous at the time so salvage crews did not go in. We have reason to believe there may be sensitive data, possible game changing information, we can extract."

"I see." Daniel rubbed his eyes. "Any idea what it might be?"

"I'd rather not speculate too much at the moment but the alliance ships were scanning the enemy vessels and may have discovered a vulnerability." Gray shrugged. "Considering our capabilities, I thought it might be worth a look. We can always just leave if it's too dangerous...and if you give me permission, I'd like to get the kielans involved too. Perform another joint operation."

"I like that idea," Daniel said. "Somewhat safe, for the most part and good for the political view. How dangerous is the sector though?"

"I don't know. We'll have to jump in on the edge, determine whether or not it's worth the risk and go in from there."

"I don't like unnecessary risks at a time like this," Daniel said. "Right on the verge of everything we're about to accomplish, it would damage relations considerably if you got yourselves killed."

"Considering our track record, I'd say losing the Behemoth is unlikely to say the least. I'd rather keep this out of the hands of the council. Can we call it a hunch and let me check? You can trust that I'll get us home safely."

Daniel considered the screen for long enough that Gray wondered if he lost the connection. When the chief spoke again, he began with a heavy sigh. "I want to give you this chance...it just could bite us both."

"Unofficially, back me up. Imagine if we find what we're looking for and if we don't, we'll just come home." Gray shrugged. "We'll even find out if there's been any activity in the area before we depart. The kielans keep record of that sort of thing."

Daniel rubbed his eyes, again thinking about it. "I would really rather say no but you wouldn't be contacting me if you didn't think this was worth the risk."

"Exactly." Gray smiled. "Think of it as recon. We're just checking out the area in and around the space we're about to share. After all, an ambassador is going to be moving out there soon. Wouldn't you think we should see how dangerous the surrounding sectors are?"

Daniel chuckled. "You really are getting good at this *explanation* thing."

"I'm paying attention."

"Indeed, you seem to be." Daniel shook his head. "Alright, you can check it out *but* do be sure that you're careful, Gray. This is literally a delicate time to be playing games. If I didn't have faith you might find something out there, I'd never allow it."

"Thank you, sir." Gray nodded. "I won't let you down."

"You haven't yet. I'm going back to bed now. Keep me informed and let the council know officially when you've accepted our membership into the alliance. Burke out."

Gray leaned back as the screen went dark. *That could've gone a lot worse*. Permission granted, he headed back to the bridge. Clea looked up sharply as he entered, her eyes full of questions. He nodded in response, taking his seat. "We have permission."

Relief washed over Clea as she seemed to deflate in her chair. "Good...I worried there for a moment."

"I played some games," Gray said. "But all around, I believe in you so I think we should check it out. Even if it doesn't have the type of information we're hoping to find, then maybe we'll find something of equal value. Either way, I look forward to checking out the space around your home world. Should give us an idea of what's happened there since you guys went to war."

"What're we talking about?" Adam asked. "Sounds like a supplemental mission to me."

"It is," Gray replied. "And I'll tell you about it over lunch. I'm starving and we're not jumping for a while. Let's grab a bite to eat and I can explain, to both of you, how I got this permission. Then, we can hop out of here and get some work done. Let's all hope for a very boring and safe trip this time out."

***

Ensign Leonard Marcus took over as the new primary navigator aboard the Behemoth. He'd been studying the position for months but only came out of the academy and boarded the ship after the incident at the research facility. He worked in one of the computer labs while they reclaimed the mining facility.

Taking a position on the bridge intimidated him but Captain Atwell told him he'd been impressed by his work after he replaced Tim Collins. Also, relieving a man because he turned traitor didn't make him feel particularly good. Still, he'd been waiting his entire life to perform such an important job and to do it before he even made lieutenant filled him with pride.

Now to live up to the task.

The kielan ship accompanying them helped with the coordinates this time. He'd only plotted simulated courses and simply double checked Tim's work before. So far, he relied on others to get the complicated work done but he didn't feel too bad about it. The fact was, he considered it on the job training.

When Captain Atwell came to Leonard's station and asked him to research a course to a set of coordinates outside of Kielan space, his pulse raced. He hadn't anticipated having to do anything until they wanted to come home and for that, he'd already read up on several good places for them to jump back to.

This was different. As he researched the area in the shared alliance database, sweat began to form on his back. The place was considered extremely dangerous. Not only was there plenty of natural debris in the area but a major battle had taken place some years back, leaving chunks of damaged ship to drift about.

Couple that with reports of pirates using it as a staging location for raids in other parts of the system made him wonder what could possibly compel them to have to go there. *And why hasn't the alliance taken care of the criminals? If they know enough to recognize they're hanging out there, they should probably step it up and get rid of them.*

Leonard checked the military reports to see if he could answer his own question. Apparently, they had gone through there a couple of times but nearly lost a ship in one of the patrols. Since then, they decided to try and find whatever haven the pirates had been using to choke them at the source.

That makes sense I suppose.

Still, it didn't explain why the Behemoth planned to go there and what they hoped to gain. Leonard wanted to ask Captain Atwell but didn't dare. Mission parameters were need to know and his job was to get them there, not quibble about why. This meant further research, which he tried to do before they jumped.

Unfortunately, their information was out of date. The ship traveling with them, which shared the database, hadn't been received an update in over two weeks. To make a jump into a place with debris and obstacles, Leonard needed something more current or they'd have to show up well outside the area.

Hours if not a full day away from anything the captain might care about. He did look over the patterns based on the information he *did* have, just to get a feel for how the junk out there moved. It didn't seem to be all that erratic and he could probably do some good math to get them there safely.

Just for the exercise, he did the work and stored his proposed coordinates. He'd do it again when they had updated data and see how close he got. As he finished up his work, Redding spoke up. "We've arrived at the jump point, sir. Leonard, are these numbers accurate and up to date?"

"Um, one moment, Ma'am." Leonard quickly checked to ensure nothing had changed. He lucked out when he received an updated set of numbers from the kielan vessel. "Received new coordinates from our allies. I've updated them in the system and we are green to go."

"Thank you, Ensign." Redding turned in her seat. "Captain, shall we go?"

"Let our friends lead the way," Captain Atwell said. "It's their home, they can open the door for us."

Leonard looked up at the view screen in time to see the kielan vessel wink out in a quick flash of white light. Jump technology fascinated him but in this particular case, he was just glad that the technicians gave their system a solid once over before they tried again. The event in their last mission made him leery of doing it again.

"They're clear," Lieutenant Darnell announced. "We're ready for departure."

"Get us out of here, Redding," Captain Atwell said.

Leonard held his breath as she acknowledged and moved her hand to the controls. Weightlessness struck him and a moment later, a single blink of the eye, he saw the kielan vessel a few thousand kilometers away. *That was the easiest our jumps have been so far! Wow, those guys really gave it some love!*

"Nicely done, everyone," Captain Atwell said. "I'm glad to not be waking up on the floor or feeling like someone tried to kick their way out of my skull. Ensign Marcus, I believe we have an eight hour flight to our destination, is that correct?"

"Um...recalculating now," Leonard said. "Looks like the flight lines are pretty clogged up right now, sir. They're asking us to take a different route. We're looking at closer to ten hours."

"Even better. I'm going to get some rest. Adam, rotate yourself and folks out as you can. We'll reconvene when we're closer. Thank you for everything you did today, people. Great, easy trip so far. There'll be a ship wide briefing before we depart and after that, everything should be fine. Ensign Marcus, do make sure you get us those coordinates I asked you about before you leave shift. Everyone else, I'll see you soon."

Chapter 4

Gray leaned back as their shuttle broke atmosphere over the kielan capital of Alantha. Even before he saw their cities or the landscape, he found himself awed by the technology they put in orbit and throughout the sector. They definitely represented a culture that had been at war for many, many years.

Defenses lined their borders, early warning systems and even weapons set to deter invasion. Ships patrolled the area, rapid response crafts which could microjump anywhere in the system at a moment's notice. The various planets around their core world housed thriving colonies, each with different methods to make the surfaces hospitable despite their distance from the sun and atmospheric conditions.

Three massive space stations made up check points throughout their solar system. One resided near to the core world while the others sat on opposite ends of the farthest reaches of their space. Each provided launch points, research facilities and supplies for expeditionary forces heading out beyond their borders.

Olly performed a scan as they arrived and provided some of the details, most of which went over Gray's head. He ultimately took away from the conversation that they built habitats Earth was only touching on, places much like the mining station they liberated only better. The amenities alone made these facilities as comfortable as any small city on Earth.

Their escort took the lead, getting them through all the challenge codes and stopping points. The ten hour trip to reach their home world provided the senior staff a chance to get some rest before what promised to be a grueling political experience. Gray put on his dress uniform before taking the bridge and when he boarded the shuttle, he brought a bag to stay the night.

He'd been told the kielans made efforts to ensure there was food appropriate to the human diet. Apparently, Clea had been making reports so they were able to ensure they got the supplies delivered in time. Some entrepreneurs even started up human cuisine restaurants for those adventurous enough to try some recipes from their new allies.

These came about a year after Clea started. Gray found it surprising they'd do so but then he looked over a brochure for one of their food courts and understood. They offered a touch of all the cultures brought into their fold but each was *their* take on the culture. Many of them could not be terribly close to accurate but Gray felt curious about what they might've done with their knowledge of Earth.

I hope they didn't adopt fast food. It couldn't possibly be good.

As they broke the clouds, he gasped, leaning to look out the window to better take in the urban sprawl of the capital. Gleaming, smooth buildings climbed into the sky and air traffic sped about at several different levels. The sky itself, where clouds didn't mar it, looked like the blue he enjoyed on Earth only a little more purple, just enough to set it apart.

Clea sat beside him, also looking out. He imagined she felt great relief at returning, considering how long she'd been gone. He turned to her, grinning. "This is fabulous. I don't know what I imagined but this exceeds my wildest expectations."

"I'm glad you like it," Clea replied, not taking her eyes away from the window. "I can't remember the last time I saw this view…but it's been a very long time. Even before I joined your crew. It's just as wondrous as I remember. Maybe made more so by distance and longing. My parents are down there somewhere, getting ready to come to the ceremony."

"I can't wait to meet them," Gray said. "What's that tall spire over there?"

"That's where our leaders congregate to legislate. The whole building acts as an antennae so they can communicate with everyone in the system, each colony and ship we have up there. If they've got speeches or information to impart, they provide it from their council chamber."

"I'm surprised how tall it is."

"Nearly two hundred stories," Clea said. "And fifteen below ground where the leaders would go if a disaster struck. People live there, government employees and such. The entire building is self contained for the most part. If they are fully supplied, they can last without outside influence for a very long time."

"Interesting, so bunkers and such...like ours."

"Yes, and you can tour it as a civilian like yours as well." Clea sighed. "Oh, it's very good to be home."

Gray leaned forward to address Redding, who piloted their shuttle down. "How're we doing?"

"Our escort says another twenty minutes for landing, sir." Redding checked a reading. "They've sent me information on all their lanes up here. Apparently, different crafts take different altitudes when traveling from place to place. All the way down to ground cars apparently. We'll be taking the top and landing at a docking bay near the capital where our ship will be searched and each of us checked to ensure we're not you know...terrorists."

"Thanks for the update." Gray leaned back. "Clea, how long do you think it'll take to get through security?"

"No longer than an hour. They're really good about it and we *are* diplomatic guests. They just have to confirm our identities and ensure we're not smuggling in a bomb or something crazy."

"Is this..." Gray checked his computer. "Ambassador Ni'Folsah going to be there?"

Clea nodded. "Undoubtedly. He'll try to speed us through the process but I can promise you security will ignore him."

Gray chuckled. "Sticklers?"

"For safety, yes. Rules...well, when it suits them."

"That works for me, I'm just thrilled to be here."

"I can't wait to show you both around. It's going to be amazing."

Gray's party consisted of Clea, Redding and four bodyguards. These were marines of the best temperament, picked by Marshall himself. Each of them dressed in dark formalwear, armed with a pistol and their long range communicators. Marshall and Captain Hoffner monitored the frequency from the Behemoth, coordinating the visit.

They were told the weapons would not be necessary by a text communication from the ambassador. No anti Earth factions existed there and no one protested the admittance of the humans to the alliance. Still, military regulations were quite specific about the protocols of an officer like Gray leaving the ship. He was to be protected against the unknown parts of any sort of event.

The air lane before them cleared out from other kielan vessels, Gray fancied them as the equivalent of police back home. They had free access to fly between massive, high tech buildings where countless kielans peered out at them as they passed. Their visit spawned a great deal of curiosity.

"They really turned out in droves," Gray said.

"Everyone does when a new culture joins us," Clea replied. "There'll be a parade at ground level tonight as part of the celebration. They'll have done as much research as they can about Earth culture to give it some flare for you. I asked Olly to pick up the broadcast and share it with the rest of the ship. They may find it interesting."

"I'm sure they'll appreciate it." Gray leaned to look past Redding again. They rapidly approached their destination where a totally empty landing pad waited. As she acknowledged some instructions he didn't hear, she spun their craft to the right and brought it in for a neat, gentle landing. "Nice landing."

"Thank you, sir. I might not be in fighter condition right now but I still hit the simulator three times a week."

"It shows." Gray disengaged the safety harness as the door opened. "Alright, everyone. Let's be sufficiently diplomatic."

Redding grinned. "I'll just follow your lead, sir."

Gray chuckled. "Thanks...considering this is my first time, I'm sure we'll both do great."

***

Clea knew security protocols with the kielan political guard and as she expected, they spent an hour going over their shuttle with sensor probes before checking them over. Ambassador Ni'Folsah complained the entire time, asking them to hurry it up and reminding them how much of a poor impression they were making.

"Safety is never a bad thing," the captain of the guard said. "And I'll ask you to wait by the door if you don't keep your mouth shut."

Clea fought hard not to grin at the indignity of the man. She'd dealt with his type only a few times before being assigned to the Behemoth and they were pains. Never wanted to follow the rules, always had an agenda they felt more important than directives and consistently threatened to escalate any request.

"Your supervisor will hear of this!" The Ambassador stomped over to the door to wait, and essentially sulk. *And there's the threat. The captain probably doesn't care one bit. He'd take more of a tongue lashing if he waved us through.*

The marines let the guards check over their weapons and had a brief conversation with them all about protocol. Some accord was reached and they were allowed to return to Gray's side. For the people, they just ran a scanner over them and frisked them. Clea came up last and the guard actually turned to his captain.

"Do we need to check her?"

"We check everyone," the captain said. *He's the stickler for the rules.* "Just get it done and we can move on with our day."

They ran the scanner over her and checked her for weapons. All she had on her was her data pad which she'd already set on their table for inspection. Their luggage would be taken inside and brought to whatever rooms they were going to be allowed to occupy. She didn't plan on staying there and would be finding her parents as soon as the ceremony ended.

Her father wanted to see the parade from ground level and they had dinner reservations afterward.

Finally, they received clearance to leave and the Ambassador rushed over with a heap of apologies. "Forgive us our paranoia," he said. "But we must be cautious in these times of war. One never knows how the insidious enemy will strike, I suppose. But the rest of your trip shall be pleasant, I assure you. We've picked out the finest suites for your rest and the council chamber is ready to receive you in a couple of hours."

"Thank you," Gray said. "We appreciate the hospitality."

"We need to check the rooms," one of the marines spoke up. "Before the captain takes it."

"Oh, of course," Ambassador Ni'Folsah said. "After our people performed their security sweep, you are more than welcome to follow whatever protocols you must. Perseverance and all. Please, take the lead with my assistant. She's going to lead us to the rooms and you can check them out."

Clea busied herself with her data pad as they boarded the elevator, sending a message to her father. "We've landed and are heading to our suites now. The ceremony is in a couple of hours. I might be able to break away just to say hi if you're in the neighborhood already. Let me know."

Before they reached their floor, she had a reply stating they were in the building and already through security joining countless others to witness Earth's admittance to the alliance first hand. "Come down if you can but be prepared for quite a crowd. If it weren't for your mother's clout with the military, I doubt we'd have a seat but we do...with an extra chair. At least for now."

"I'll see you soon." She felt anxious to get down there and as the elevator opened, she had to fight not to hurry. So long away from family and friends, she hadn't realized just how much she missed them. Now that she had the chance to see them again, she practically wanted to jump out of her skin to get there as soon as possible.

The marines swept through Gray's suite but she and Redding were allowed to go into theirs. Clea stepped inside, washed her face and came back out to find the captain still waiting. "Sir, if you don't mind, I'd like to go down to the lobby. My parents are already here. I'll be back in time for the ceremony."

Gray gestured down the hall. "Please, get going. I'll see you in a while."

Clea smiled brightly. "Thank you, sir. See you soon."

She practically jogged down the hall and hit the button, suppressing an urge to bounce on the balls of her feet. As the elevator arrived, she boarded and tapped the lobby button several times before leaning back against the wall. She was alone for the first two floors but by the time she got to her destination, people got on and left ten times. Nearly eight people stood in front of her as the doors opened to the lobby.

Moving off with them, she shuffled toward a massive crowd, one of the biggest she'd ever seen on her world. Taking out her pad, she texted her father, "I'm in the lobby. Where should I go?"

"We're about twenty meters from the monitors on the right side of the room if you're facing away from the front doors. I'll stand up and wave."

Clea looked over the crowd and most of them were standing. She wasn't the shortest kielan but many of these folks towered over her. *I doubt I'll see him waving. Okay, I'll just shove my way through the area and see what I can do.*

The monitors were mounted high up in the room so everyone had a good vantage. She marked the one she needed and hurried off, excusing herself through the crowd. It took a good five minutes to locate their table but when she saw her parents, her heart hammered hard in her chest.

"Hello!" Clea cried out, waving over her head. Her mother, who she favored with the same silver-blue eyes and nearly black-purple hair, just appeared a bit older, extended her arms and they embraced. "I missed you so much!"

"We've missed you too!" Her mother said. "Oh, you look fabulous! And a su-anthar now! We're so proud of you!"

Clea blushed. "Thank you..." Her father clapped her shoulder before embracing her. He looked a bit older than the last time she saw him, with some additional lines around his gray-green eyes. His once vibrant, lighter purple hair, lost most of its color, turning a striking white. "You both looked great."

"Yes, well, it's been a less active few years for us than you," her father said. "We've followed your exploits and you've been quite busy. No wonder you were able to secure your rank. You've been performing."

"I can't even believe all we've done so far but...I haven't told them about what typically happens when a culture's admitted to the alliance."

Her father's brows went up. "They don't know you may be reassigned?"

Clea shook her head. "No, but I looked and I have the authority to request I stay on...and continue to serve with them for a time."

"You do," her mother replied, "but will you?"

"I believe so. I've done so much with them, distinguished myself...I think there's more to be done."

"But you'll be back at Earth," her father said. "Again."

"I know, father. But it hopefully won't be much longer."

"And on a ship of the line," her mother pointed out. "Very dangerous."

"It's dangerous anywhere but here and even this place, I don't know. If the enemy decided to attempt a full scale invasion?"

"Intelligence suggests they don't know our exact coordinates," her father said. "Though I'm not counting on that entirely."

"Exactly. I feel strongly that we need to take the fight to them if we hope to win." Clea thought back to her dream. She wanted to bring it up to them but it didn't seem like the time. Maybe over dinner when there weren't so many people around. "I...wanted to tell you how sorry I am about Vora."

Her father's face turned grim and he shook his head. "Don't be. It wasn't your fault and you did *exactly* what you had to. Vora made her choice."

Her mother looked on the verge of tears. "I still don't understand what she was thinking. She refused to see us when they brought her back here for trial. I'm hoping before the sentencing, she'll want to talk."

"I doubt she'll have anything we want to hear," her father said. "I wouldn't count on her being particularly forthcoming with motives that make any sense."

"I can attest she won't," Clea said. "We talked...a few times. She admits she was wrong now. Her reasons...she was always arrogant but this...this went above and beyond. It was treason without logical direction."

"I understand the humans just had to deal with some betrayal of their own," her mother said.

"How do you know that?"

Her mother grinned. "I spent nearly twenty years working with intelligence. I still get some of the briefings, especially about the ship my daughter's serving on."

Clea smirked. "Well, then you know more than I do I assume. Two young men and a woman accepted orders from a superior to damage relations between the alliance and Earth. They initially wanted to frame me but it didn't work out."

"Deplorable behavior," he father said. "They could learn a few things about self preservation. It should be part of the criteria to admittance. That right there should've been good reason to deny them another six months or year."

"Father, we need all the help we can get right now and denial would've set things back on all sides. Giving a victory to their separatist faction wouldn't have done anyone any good."

"Perhaps not," her father replied. "But I'm not entirely convinced they're to be trusted after this. Of course, we're far more forgiving of that sort of thing. It's the individual, not the culture, which makes a decision such as this. I just hope it does not bite us this time. From everything I've read, they're a fairly warlike culture."

"Historically, true." Clea nodded. "But they've got a lot of positive things too. Their art is fabulous and they care very much about their history."

"It teaches them how to fight better," her mother said.

"But not just that," Clea continued, "they remember the glories of their scientists and creators as well. All around, the humans have a complex culture. One that we can learn from…just as they can learn from us. After serving closely with them for so long, I can say they have their faults but their virtues far outweigh them."

Her mother cupped her cheek. "You truly have become the ambassador for them they needed. I hope they realize how lucky they are to have you."

Clea winked, "sometimes, I make it clear."

"Well, let's catch up on less serious matters," her mother said. "I'm sure we can find something frivolous to talk about. For instance, I planted a new garden on the south side of the back lawn. Mostly spices and herbs. I think you'd love the way it smells. And your Aunt Vina just bought me a new weather station that's vastly superior to my old one."

Clea let out a contented sigh and enjoyed the moment with her family. She knew she'd have a few days with them, perhaps longer but their initial gathering felt perfect. This was what she needed and didn't even know it. A chance to simply be with them and enjoy *real* time off. Later, they'd really get a chance to talk but until dinner, this was exactly what she needed.

***

Gray met with the ambassador and went through the semantics of the ceremony. He would arrive in the council chamber with his two attendants, in this case Redding and Clea, then approach by himself. The head councilman, Malan Dor'Aval, would recite a passage. They would then hand him a ceremonial baton, a symbol of Earth's stake in the alliance.

The ritual of it seemed simple enough. Gray had been through enough military traditions to understand. He felt thankful all he had to do was say *thank you* and *I accept*. Once they finished, those gathered would applaud and Gray would be out to watch the parade. When that finished, he had an invitation from the military councilmen for dinner *then* he could get some rest.

Clea planned to spend the evening with her family and Redding planned to join him for the shop talk. Various minor details needed to be worked out before one of Earth's politicians and the real ambassador arrived to take their post. Then they'd be able to visit the discussion of claiming the salvage.

I hope they get behind this. She's pretty passionate about what we'll find.

Gray arrived at the council chamber a little early and felt tremendous awe as he peered inside. The room had a hundred foot ceiling and all around men and women gathered to watch the ceremony. All the leaders sat in an elevated dais some twenty feet above the floor. An attendant, the man carrying the baton, would be on the same level as the visitors.

The metal appeared to be shiny gold, glimmering from subtle lights hidden in recessed tracks all about the room. He backed into the antechamber with the ambassador and checked his chronometer. They had a good ten minutes before the event started but neither Clea nor Redding had arrived yet.

"They'll be here," Gray said. "I'm sure the crowds have kept them."

"We should've had them stay with us," Ni'Folsah said. "We do not want to delay things."

"You won't," Redding announced as she and Clea approached. "The elevator was terrible. Stopped on every floor."

"Thank goodness you made it." Ni'Folsah looked like he might faint he was so relieved. "This is a momentous occasion, one we do not want to mess up with tardiness."

"We understand, sir." Clea bowed her head. "I look forward to participating."

He went over the process again with them and Gray noted he recited it the *exact* same way. *Like an actor I guess. This is all a show, after all.* The others listened patiently, probably wondering why they needed to understand it all when they just needed to stand around. At least he made them feel included.

Suddenly, the crowd fell silent. The council arrived to the sound of a massive gong. Gray peeked out and saw the five people take their seats on the dais. Their attendant positioned himself behind a podium, clasping his hands behind his back. Guards took up position around all the exits. Redding glanced at him, leaning close to whisper.

"This is intense."

"It really is," Gray replied. "I can't wait to see how they give the speech."

"Don't forget," Ni'Folsah said, "they will start in our language and then welcome you in yours."

"I hope I don't need to know what they're saying," Redding replied.

"You don't," Gray said. "I've got an earpiece to translate."

The gong sounded again. Ni'Folsah tapped Gray's arm and gestured. "Go ahead, sir! Go ahead!"

Gray paced out before the dais with Clea and Redding close behind. He stood at attention, looking up at the council as they prepared to address them. Though there were innumerable people watching, it felt as though the setting were somehow intimate, that the men above and the Behemoth crew were the only ones present.

The words translated in his ear.

"We have gathered to bring to the fold another culture, one full of differences and nuances, their own beliefs and goals. These unique attributes when combined with ours shall make the entirety of our alliance stronger. As we grow, so will our enemies shrink. We work toward the same goal, suppression of war and expansion of exploration.

"There are other cultures, other galaxies to unite in commonality and peace. The future holds many discoveries, many mysteries we have yet to unravel. These journeys, yet unplanned or imagined, are far better when undertaken with friends. Together, with our combined strength, we shall make our collective alliance stable, wise and ever vigilant."

He shifted his words to English, looking directly at Gray.

"You represent the Earth and your exploits are well known to us. We have read the reports and stand impressed. Through the years, you have stood on your own against a tide of darkness with increasing help and cooperation from the kielan people. Now, as you join us here as partners, your patience and perseverance have paid off."

"Thank you, sir," Gray replied, bowing his head briefly.

"We offer you a great responsibility, one we believe you are more than capable of shouldering. Each mission has shown we are making the right decision." The attendant suddenly advanced, holding out the baton. "We extend this token as a representation of our will that we wish you to join us, that you take up the torch of our cause and make it your own, just as we do the same for you.

"Of these things and all we have to offer, do you, Captain Gray Atwell of the Planet Earth, accept this responsibility on behalf of your species, military and political bodies?"

"I accept." Gray intoned. He took the baton as it was offered.

"So by taking up the item, you too are now part of the alliance. Welcome, new friends. May we have many years of peace, cooperation and prosperity."

The applauds were incredible, near deafening as thousands of people clapped their hands and shouted their excitement. Gray couldn't help but be moved, his heart rate picking up and his body trembling. The weight of so many people staring at them weighed on him and he stood with his head high throughout the conclusion.

The rest of the night would be considerably less intense but that moment, he embraced the spectacle of it. Few people could claim to be part of history, to participate in something schools would teach for years to come. He was proud to consider what his contribution provided to his people, his friends and culture.

Redding shook his hand then Clea as well. The council bowed as they departed. The ambassador ushered them through the door and back out into the chamber. The parade would begin any moment and he had a perfect seat for him and Redding to enjoy it. A few hours of celebration felt right after such a solemn affair.

And afterward, they could truly focus on ending the conflict plaguing all the universe and get back to the real purpose of space travel: exploration and peace.

Chapter 5

The time spent on Alantha went by in a whirlwind for Gray. He witnessed the parade then immediately was swept off to dinner and late night conversation with the military council. He felt they hit it off well and he enjoyed their company. It would make his conversation with them later much easier.

Afterward, he took a tour with the ambassador but assumed it would be the safe version, not like what Clea might offer. He didn't see her for the first two days. She went and stayed with her family before linking up with him the morning of the third day. Redding accompanied them and she gave them the insider trip, showing them places off the beaten path.

On the fourth day, Gray met with the head of the military, essentially Daniel Burke's equivalent. His name was Dane G'ursa, an older kielan who still looked like he was in his forties. *I hope I age even half as well. These guys must have an amazing diet.* They sat in a cozy den off one of the spire's main passage ways.

"So Captain," Dane said, "what is it you wish to discuss?"

"We're interested in the salvage of a battle that took place some time ago," Gray explained. "You fought against four enemy ships and destroyed them all but unfortunately lost a couple of your own."

"Salvage?" Dane's brows lifted. "I'm not sure what you mean. If it was an older fight, what do you hope to find?"

"It's a dangerous area." Gray offered him his data pad so Dane could see the location in question. "We believe that anyone who has been through there might not have gotten what we're after."

"So my question still stands."

"We think there's information about the enemy...something vital."

"It would be a shame if we left it behind." Dane handed back the pad and rubbed his chin. "I do know the area. My son fought in that battle, on a ship that was not damaged. What do you need from us? Surely if you were going to check it out, you must've realized we would not have stopped you."

"It's not that," Gray said. "We're hoping to cooperate...to get a little help."

"I see. What sort?"

Gray hesitated a moment, thinking through what they really needed. He didn't want another captain there cutting into the operation. Maybe something small would work better. Enough to show they were working together but not enough to limit their ability to react to the situation as he saw fit.

"A tech crew would be nice," Gray said. "We need some folks to supplement Su-Anthar An'Tufal's knowledge of this technology so we can properly investigate what we discover."

Dane nodded. "I believe we can do that quite easily." He got out a computer pad of his own and tapped out a message. "I'll have them report to the Behemoth in the next two days. They'll bring a jump capable shuttle...just in case."

"They have to leave in a hurry?" Gray asked.

Dane shrugged. "One never knows what one will find in forgotten sectors. It's best to be prepared. Is there anything else you wish to discuss?"

"No, I think we're good. Unless you'd like another round of cultural exchange."

Dane smiled brightly and nodded. "I would. I'll start, this time with breakfast rituals..."

***

Clea got the message from Gray stating the kielans committed to helping with the salvage operation. She was sitting with her parents in the house, having breakfast. Her mother took her hand gently and brought her back to reality. She hadn't even realized she'd been staring off into space.

"What is it?"

Clea smiled. "Just thinking about my first combat mission."

"That was a bad one," her father said. "You were in the hospital for a few days. Never wanted to talk about it."

"Do you want to now?" her mother looked worried.

"No, not really. I guess I just didn't realize how much it effected me. I've been thinking about it a lot lately."

"Why?" Her father asked. "Any particular reason?"

"I had a crazy dream...and when I woke up, I remembered a bunch of details. The psychologist told me that might happen but after a few years, I figured he was wrong."

"They rarely are." Her father squinted at her. "So what are you going to do?"

"I convinced Captain Atwell to take a trip out to the battle site," Clea said. "We're going to see if there's anything to salvage of my old station."

Her father nodded. "What do you hope to find?"

"A key to helping fight the enemy," Clea replied. "A way to drive them back maybe...I don't know. Something about my past so I can put this behind me maybe? But I don't think I'm that selfish. I genuinely believe I found something while we were on that mission and I want to be sure I explore the option."

"Then you're being thorough," her mother said, "and that's a good trait."

"I hope so." Clea sighed. "I have to go back to the ship tomorrow morning."

"And you'll be off?" Her father asked.

Clea nodded.

"Then today, we'll stay in and be together," her mother squeezed her hand. "Who knows the next time we'll see one another?"

"Who indeed?" Clea muttered. "I like that plan, guys. Thank you."

"Any time, daughter." Her father patted her shoulder. "Any time."

***

Gray received access to a library with accounts of space battles conducted by the kielans throughout the war. These were simulations a commander could watch from any angle and study the tactics to better understand the forces they were up against. Some of the losses were also recorded, pieced together through scans and collection of salvage.

He watched a couple of these early in the morning while having breakfast. The ability to move the camera to any point and witness the fight from different perspectives appealed to his tactical mind. The kielans in particular were cunning with their use of microjumps and focused firepower from multiple vessels.

After going through several of the fights, he brought up the one that destroyed the ship Clea was on with the data they needed. The conflict was old and the computer spent almost a minute updating the graphics to modern thresholds. When it fully loaded, he put in his ear bud and hit play, watching from the perspective of the four alliance battleships.

It seems odd to be watching a fight when someone I knew was there. Incredible.

The battle started out with the four enemy vessels jumping into the area at nearly five hundred thousand kilometers out. The eight alliance ships separated, spacing themselves out distant enough that splash damage would not be a concern. Shields went up and they advanced, preparing for what appeared to be a toe to toe struggle.

The ship on the outer most starboard side suddenly performed a micro jump and hit one of the enemies on the flank. They began to exchange fire while the rest of the alliance ships focused all their attention on the outer most vessel on the opposite side. Concentrated fire pounded the enemy's shields but this was back when the alliance was technically outmatched.

An energy build up launched a blast into one of the seven alliance ships working together, punching right through its shields. Gray saw what they did. Right when the kielans fired, the enemy hit them while their power dipped from weapon discharge. It caused hull damage and a follow up shot finished them off.

They worked down the shields and caused catastrophic damage to their enemy, destroying their engines first then causing fractures all across the hull. They didn't have data to support it, but Gray figured he just witnessed the entire ship lose artificial atmosphere, possibly killing everyone board.

If they didn't matter whether they survived that initial damage or not. Moments later, the entire vessel exploded, leaving behind little more than debris.

Fighters joined the fray, screaming about and engaging hostiles. Some got through and hit another of the kielan vessels, causing shield damage enough for the larger of the enemy ships to fire a blast and knock out its defenses. Gray took a moment to observe that ship. He hadn't seen such a large one in their fights so far and certainly not one that hung back.

The kielans managed to destroy another enemy with continuous pulse bursts over the upper part of the enemy hull. They performed flybys and microjumped to safety. Their fighters managed to finish one off, obliterating it with bombs before turning to the next. Sadly, those ships were taken out by enemy fighters.

Their exchange of damages was brutal and constant. Each side vied for more catastrophic damage and as another kielan vessel exploded, Gray tensed up. They'd brought down two of the enemy ships and a third was suffering under heavy damage. The *Tempered Steel* went up next, a shot tearing through its hull and splitting it down the center.

Clea's vessel. Gray couldn't believe anyone survived the attack. While the ship itself was not obliterated, several holes appeared throughout the hull. The fact so many people got off the ship was a testament to their safety protocols and quick thinking. Some of it was luck too, because if that had hit a different way, they'd all be gone.

I wonder if Clea has watched this.

The last five ships were able to dispatch the damaged enemy. They went for what they assumed was the bridge, according to the text at the bottom of the screen. Each vessel flanked and went to town, hitting it with everything they had. When it finally drifted off and exploded, the larger ship jumped out of the system and the kielans started search and rescue operations took another six hours to complete.

Holy crap, those people required aid for an entire shift! Amazing.

Gray understood why they might've lost the equipment then. By the time they finished their rescue operations, they received a signal of more enemies incoming. They jumped out to report in and lick their wounds. Another engagement in the area took place but between the enemy and a different culture. He didn't know how it ended.

Why was the enemy so interested in that space?

He checked the area and discovered the sector happened to be adjacent to several others with settlements and resource rich planets. Perhaps they were expanding for that reason but every engagement left both sides off poorly. Eventually, they seemed to stop but not before dozens of ships were destroyed in the area.

It's the Bermuda Triangle of space.

Gray shut down the computer and went about his day but he couldn't shake the fight out of his head. Eight against four and they lost three vessels. He fought two enemy vessels with the aid of a ship that wasn't even fully operational and won, albeit not easily. Of course, the years apart in the conflict made a difference. Technology was a lot better already.

Still, the first days of the war must've been terrifying. Such heavy losses couldn't have been easy to bear. *I hope you found something out there, Clea. This has to stop. One way or another, it has to stop.*

***

Adam joined Group Commander Estaban Revente in the hangar as the kielan shuttle came aboard. The two men watched as the shiny craft came to a rest in the middle of the deck, air bursting from the landing gear as it settled. Deck crew hurried over and locked it down, ensuring it would not move in the event of a gravity shift.

"Looks pretty," Adam said. "The captain's message said it's jump capable."

"I didn't even know smaller ships *could* jump," Estaban said. "Amazing, huh? I look forward to a tour of the thing."

"I'm sure they'll hook you up eventually." Adam checked his chronometer. "I have to get to the bridge. The captain's landing in ten minutes and he wants us underway within the hour. You find someone who can maneuver around all that debris?"

"I've narrowed it down to Pointer or Hale," Estaban said. "Whichever of them wants to go."

"Maybe they should both do it," Adam pointed out. "They'll need a copilot, someone good enough to take over if necessary."

Estaban grinned. "Trying to take my job, Commander?"

Adam chuckled. "Not at all. I'll leave you to it then." He headed back to the bridge and took a seat. Olly sat at his station, tapping away. Redding returned before Gray and she was already back on duty, working with Leonard to get them safe passage out of the system. When the captain boarded, they'd be off to their next mission.

"How're we doing, everyone?"

"We're ready to depart," Redding said. "Leonard has plotted a solid jump course."

` "How close was it to your initial estimates?" Adam asked.

Leonard turned and smiled. "I was off by less than three hundred meters…a very reasonable margin and one which would've worked just fine."

"Congratulations and good job on the great math." Adam checked his computer for reports. All stations showed green. "Time to get back to action, folks. I hope you're ready."

"Not much action to be found in salvage," Olly said.

"When was the last time something went right?" Redding countered.

Olly blushed. "Good point." He paused. "Captain's shuttle is landing now."

Adam brought Gray up on his com. "You here, sir?"

"I am, Adam. Get us moving."

"Aye, captain." Adam turned to the others. "Agatha, do we have clearance to depart?"

"We do, sir. Our window of opportunity is now."

"Take us out, Redding."

"Yes, sir." Redding initiated the thrusters and they began to move, rumbling at first then smoothing out. They pulled away from orbit and headed toward open space. "We will be at the jump point in less than two hours."

"Sounds good." Adam turned to Olly. "You might want to hop down and familiarize yourself with the technicians who just came on board. I suspect you'll be working closely with them throughout this operation."

"I will, sir. Is Miss An'Tufal going to be there?"

"Yes, she came aboard with the captain. Grab her on the way. You've got two hours to get ready for the op. I suggest anyone who has a part to play double check that they're ready. If this place is as dangerous as the reports suggest, we're going to need to be on our toes the entire time."

***

Despite the success of their last jump, Redding still didn't entirely trust their faster than light travel. It burned them too many times and would definitely have to earn back her faith. She didn't hesitate to initiate the process but her stomach tightened up seconds before they made the trip.

When they appeared without incident, not even a strange feeling, she sighed and refocused on her job. *Two for two so far. They really did seem to fix it.*

Olly put the sector up on the main screen, showing a massive field of rock and chunks of ship. There were far more than the two enemies and three alliance vessels. This was a graveyard for starships of all sizes. More than a few battles took place there and they didn't seem to go very well for most of the participants.

Gray spoke up, directing his attention to Clea. "I read the briefing that this place was dangerous but…what happened here? Why so many battles? Why so much debris?"

"Long ago, a planet became unstable and essentially exploded," Clea explained. "This made for excellent mining. Before the enemy attacked, many cultures even within the alliance fought over the rights to claim the minerals. Pirates got involved back then as well. Then the enemy attacked and since then, I'm not aware of any further conflict."

"Did the mining dry up?" Redding asked.

"Not really. Those who risk coming out here don't fight amongst themselves. They only really have to worry about criminals and if they see some coming, they can just flee. Of course, some fights like that would not be reported to alliance command so...maybe they blast away at each other all the time."

"I'm picking up a group of ships," Olly said. "Not far off. They seem to be scouring the wreckage...over there." He focused the screen on a section off to the left. "Looks like five total."

Redding leaned forward to look. "Those aren't alliance."

"They used to be," Clea said. "Those, my friends, are pirates."

Gray replied, "wonderful. Olly, get us a good scan of those vessels. If we have to engage, I'd like to be prepared."

"Yes, sir."

A readout of the largest one, essentially the size of a scout, appeared on the screen. Redding estimated it had a crew of thirty with room for maybe four fighters. It was armed with modern weapons so not as helpless as the new culture they encountered. Still, they were so small any hit from the pulse cannons would likely eliminate them.

The others were like large shuttles. Olly posted on the screen that they probably attached themselves to the hull of the larger one when they weren't performing an operation. Redding waited for the order to approach, feeling particularly ready to throw down with these guys. The pirates at the mining facility left a bad taste in her mouth.

"I'm picking up a communication," Agatha announced. "They've hailed us, asking for our immediate surrender."

Redding's eyes widened and she turned to look back at Gray. He wore an equal look of surprise. "They must not have very good scans."

"They did hit us with one," Olly said. "Maybe they only got a cursory look at what we've got going on."

"We should finish them off," Clea said. "Take them down so we don't have to worry about them stinging us while we perform our search."

"I agree," Adam added. "Hitting them hard and fast will get them out of the way before they can fly off and get lost in this mess but we shouldn't risk fighters out in that. These guys look like they've been here a while. They might know the area better...and all the places to maneuver to avoid collisions."

"Agatha," Gray began, "no reply. Redding, advance. Weapons hot. Let's get our shields up."

"Weapons fully charged and ready," Redding said. "Maximum range in twenty seconds. Optimal in one minute."

"Shields are online," Olly said.

"Sound the alert," Gray added.

Red lights went on behind Redding and she did her best to ignore them. The targeting computer assisted her with lining up decent shots, grabbing each of the vessels with a different turret. The scout might be able to survive a direct hit or two but the others would go down almost instantly.

"Optimal range achieved," Redding announced. "Permission to open fire."

"Granted," Gray said. "Take them out."

Redding pulled the trigger, letting the various turrets rip. The scout took a direct hit to the port side, near their engines and another barely ten meters up. One of the shuttles was gone in a globe of red fire while two more took direct hits and began to drift. A fourth managed to dodge the attack and attempted to fly into the wreckage.

Redding redirected a turret and opened fire, scoring a hit to the engines. Another one exploded, pieces of the ship flying in all directions.

The scout vessel returned fire, a continuous beam that struck the Behemoth's shields for a good ten seconds. Olly's hands moved so fast he distracted Redding for a moment and she took a quick glance. He looked frantic, actually worried. Whatever they had might actually be far more dangerous than they anticipated.

"That thing just dropped our shields from one hundred percent to *ten* percent!"

"In that section?" Gray asked.

"No, sir. *All* our shields are at ten percent!"

"Impossible!" Adam nearly shouted. "How the hell...what kind of weapon is that?"

"Analyzing it now."

"At least we know why they demanded our surrender," Gray said. "Redding, finish that ship off right now."

"Yes, sir." She directed all their weapons on the target, opening up with everything. It would require a recharge when they were done but it didn't seem like keeping available weapons was as important as removing that threat. Every blast scored a direct hit, tearing through the scout's shields and wreaking havoc over its hull.

A piece of debris collided with it as their weapons forced the thing off course. A crack appeared in the hull and a moment later, the entire thing went up and burst. Once again, pieces were cast off to join the rest of the wreckage, another ship for this boneyard. *I understand why they risk this place. It's a wealth of salvage.*

"Captain," Agatha spoke up. "The final shuttle is transmitting to us again. They wish to surrender, sir. They've cut all power to their weapons and are drifting."

"Olly?"

"Scanning them now." Olly tapped his console impatiently. "There we go. It looks like they're telling the truth. They've turned their offensive systems *off.* They're not on standby."

"Okay, tell them we need access to their computer systems immediately and we'll bring them aboard."

Olly spent the next few minutes disabling their systems before they allowed them to land. Marines were dispatched to take the prisoners to the brig. This allowed them to refocus on the whole purpose of going there. They needed to find this ship that Clea served on but after seeing the mess out there, Redding had no idea how they planned to do so.

"How're our shields now?" Gray asked.

"Recharging, sir," Olly replied. "I'd love to get a look at that weapon. I don't think it's intact though."

"Ya think?" Redding muttered.

"Start the scans for the *Tempered Steel*," Gray said. "Clea and the tech team will assist. Remember, we're in a hostile environment. That's bad enough without being shot at so keep yourselves frosty and let's get out of here without injury or damage."

***

Clea worked closely with Olly, Paul and the keilan tech crew to start a sensor web looking for the old wreckage. They collected massive amounts of data and each of them began processing it as quickly as possible. Over an hour later, they still hadn't found what they were looking for and only analyzed half of their information.

They did, however, catalog a number of items worth investigating later. Much had been stripped though and Clea started worrying about what they'd find at the *Tempered Steel*. It may not be there at all, stripped of all but the frame itself. She tried to prepare herself for that eventuality but couldn't quite shake the despair.

Another half hour later, Paul shouted out to them. "I found it!"

Olly and Clea joined him while the others continued to work. There'd been enough false positives that not everyone got excited from a find. The three of them peered over the screen and Clea really scrutinized his findings. The mass and density were correct so it may at least have been one of the vessels they lost.

If it's not the Steel, it's going to be close to it. We haven't lost that many ships out here.

The hulk didn't radiate any power, it was certainly dead. That meant they could not remotely claim any data from whatever storage banks might be left. They'd have to physically visit the wreckage and take things the old fashioned way. Luckily, the tech team brought cutting torches capable of removing bulk heads.

"I'll tell the captain," Clea said. "Keep analyzing the data until we're ready to do something about this."

Clea left, rushing to the elevator and hurrying along the hall to the bridge. She stormed in, causing Leonard to jump. "Welcome back," Adam grumbled. "You're excited."

"We found alliance wreckage," Clea replied, breathing heavily from her run. "There's no power out there so we'll have to go there."

"The Behemoth can't make that trip," Gray said. "We'd probably make it even more hazardous, pushing all that debris around."

Clea nodded. "We'll bring the shuttle. It's got the shields for it and can maneuver the way the pirates did."

"You're going to need someone particularly good at flying," Adam said. "One of the bomber pilots maybe. Someone who can handle a bigger craft."

"Rudy," Gray said. "He's got the chops for this. Have Revente send him down."

Clea stood at attention. "Sir, I would like to accompany the team."

"Clea, that's probably not a good idea." Gray frowned. "Let's talk in the ready room."

The two of them disappeared into his office and closed the door. He turned to her and kept his voice low. "Sometimes, it's important for a superior officer to let their subordinates do their jobs. You can't hover over them all the time."

"I trust them all, of course," Clea said. "But I want to see it with my own eyes...to be there again and...I don't know...put my memories to rest I suppose. Besides, I know *exactly* where we have to look and they'd flounder."

"You can't show them on a schematic?"

"The ship's been cut in half and is possibly worse by now. I'm afraid there won't be a map for however many sections it's been broken into."

"I shouldn't permit this."

"I hope you will."

Gray stepped away, peering at a monitor for several long moments. Clea worried he would come back with a negative but she didn't see the harm in her departure. She'd gone down to the research facility after all. Why not a jaunt into space? Her zero G qualification was still current.

"Okay, Clea, you can go."

Clea closed her eyes in silent thanks.

"Providing you be careful. I can't afford to lose our liaison. You're lucky I'm not as conservative as the rest of my military council."

"I appreciate your confidence, sir. We'll return with what we're after or bad news. Either way, I believe this is something I need to do…for my sanity."

"I hope it helps. Be safe, Su-Anthar. I look forward to your report."

Clea gave him a salute. "Yes, sir." And departed the bridge.

***

Rudy arrived at the flight deck and looked over the shuttle they expected him to fly. The tech crew who brought the thing were all certified pilots but none of them actually had experience in the sort of environment they were about to fly through. Revente told him to consider it a combat op but that made him nervous.

He never used kielan technology. Their own bombers were *human* designed *based* on alliance work. This thing...he hoped they kept it pretty straightforward or he'd be telling them he wasn't their guy. As he boarded the ship, he noted that the cargo area had been converted into a computer lab but the walls represented every other military vehicle he'd ever been on.

Spartan and bare. At least these guys aren't all flash and pomp.

Rudy climbed a ladder up to the next section, a living space with eight bunks recessed into the walls, two by two. At the end, a hatch led to a mess area then the bridge was another ten meters away. *This isn't a shuttle, it's an RV for scientists*. He figured they could carry enough supplies to survive for weeks if not a full month in deep space.

Not exactly luxury but doable.

Taking a look at the controls, he let out a sigh of relief. Flight controls looked a lot like his bomber with a throttler on the right and wheel in front. One of the techs joined him. "Hello there. My name's Arak."

"Rudy, nice to meet you."

"Indeed." Arak smiled. "Can I give you a brief tour of the pilot's station?"

"Go for it," Rudy replied.

The primer was more than sufficient to get him up to snuff but he didn't quite feel comfortable flying a combat mission in it. Arak stated he'd be riding co-pilot to help with shield control and navigation. Plus, Rudy would have a good twenty minutes to get the feel of the ship before they arrived at the debris field.

Plenty of time. I hope.

Clea joined them, carrying a large case. "There are more of these in the back in the event that we have to leave the shuttle."

"What are they?" Rudy asked.

"Environmental suits. I have a feeling we're going to have to physically check out the wreckage to find what we're after."

"Oh…" Rudy nodded, suddenly grateful he'd be up in the front of the ship flying it. "Good luck with that."

"I appreciate that, Wing Commander." Clea turned to Arak. "Can we change in the mess area?"

"There are a couple of rooms down there where you can have some privacy," Arak said. "Go ahead."

"Thank you. Rudy, we leave in fifteen minutes."

"Let me just grab my things and I'll start our preflight check."

Rudy stowed his gear behind the seat and ran through the various systems with Arak, ensuring they were ready to go. Everything checked out and he contacted the tower. They gave him immediate clearance and a few moments later, the hangar deck cleared. His communicator went off, a private message from Revente.

"You sure you got this, Hale?"

"Yes, sir. I just went over it with one of theirs. The ship's enough like ours to make it okay."

"Be very careful out there. I looked at the scans and you're flying into some of the worst environmental hazards I've ever seen."

"Sounds like a challenge."

"Just make sure you don't take unnecessary risks. Revente out."

Very inspirational. Thank you for that, Commander.

Clea returned wearing all but the helmet of an environmental suit. It fit the body tightly with rigid plates in place to avoid damage. A wrist computer attached to her left arm and a small pack rested on her back. He'd seen one of the kielan suits before and knew that they had a continuous oxygen generator that took up the bottom of the burden. Anything else in there must've been to enhance the computer.

"Okay, Mister Hale," Clea said. "I believe everyone's ready. You can take us out."

"Yes, Ma'am." Rudy took a deep breath and engaged the engines. The ship rumbled as he turned it around slowly, bringing them out of the hangar into deep space. *Here we go. Learn fast, Hale. You don't have time for mistakes.*

Chapter 6

Rudy took the ship through some paces as they departed the Behemoth, getting a feel for how the thrusters moved them about. The inertial dampeners were incredible, reacting to the twitchiest motions he could manage. As they pulled a lazy circle, he felt confident he could get them where they needed to go.

"If you're ready," Clea said, "I've put the information up on your screen. Just follow the marker and we'll be in the general vicinity."

"Yes, Ma'am." Rudy narrowed his eyes and read the scanner. Revente wasn't kidding. The debris he saw made his stomach turn. *This place is insane!*

"I'm increasing power to the shields," Arak said. "I don't think all the debris will be avoidable. Just the biggest of them."

Rudy nodded, concentrating for their entry into the field far too much to reply. He saw a massive bulkhead floating less than two hundred meters off to the starboard. Directly ahead, small rocks probably the size of his fist were highlighted by the scanner. He slowed down and nudged them with the shields, entering the area at little more than a drift.

"Subtle flying," Arak said. "I'm quite impressed."

"Thanks," Rudy muttered. "I didn't know I had it in me."

"Mister Hale is a bomber pilot," Clea explained. "Which means subtlety isn't usually part of his job."

"Ah." Arak nodded, turning back to his station. "We've got a massive asteroid to port drifting toward us. Without compensation, it'll collide in less than a minute."

Wow, this guy's pretty calm considering what that would mean. Rudy compensated by initiating the thrusters, pushing them starboard to avoid the thing. He turned and saw it, swallowing hard. The *massive asteroid* might've been half the size of the Behemoth. It would've been like being on a raft and getting crushed by a humpback whale.

I guess I'm glad he didn't start yelling. They've got some faith in me I guess.

Rudy climbed to avoid a particularly dense patch of technical debris, pieces of ship that he couldn't identify. They moved past it and ever deeper into the field. He checked the scanner just to scare himself, to see how far they were away from the Behemoth and they'd already traveled over ten-thousand kilometers. Twenty minutes had passed.

That long? It felt like five.

A near miss nearly shaved their underside but he managed to twitch up, avoiding that asteroid but connecting with a few small rocks directly above them. The shields deflected them but Arak warned they dropped to forty-percent. Rudy let them recharge before pressing on, trying to take more care with the scanners.

"I'm picking up a small vessel," Arak said. "Roughly equivalent to us moving in."

"On intercept?" Rudy asked. "Out here?"

"The pirates fight in this sector all the time," Arak replied. "I would not be surprised if they assume we're just some competition."

"Do we have any weapons?" Rudy assumed they did but the question made sense.

"Indeed. Pulse cannons and military grade missiles."

Rudy nodded. "Great. Should we contact them first? Give them a chance to back off?"

Clea spoke up, "there's a good chance they'll ignore us but I agree. Out here, in this mess, it would be best to avoid a fight."

Rudy engaged the communicator and tried to hail the craft. "Attention, incoming vessel. This is Commander Hale on an alliance salvage run. Please fall back and disengage. We are *not* here for a fight."

"They're maintaining course," Arak said.

"C'mon, guys. Do you really want to throw down out here? We're looking for one thing and you can go back to whatever you're doing."

"Alliance ship," a man's voice crackled through the speakers. "This is the *Dragon's Tongue* and you're infringing on our territory. If you don't want to be obliterated, fall back now and get out of this sector. This is your one and only warning."

"Did you totally ignore what I just said?" Rudy asked. "We're *alliance*. That means military and we're not infringing on anything. You can't claim this junkyard. Half the stuff out here belongs to us. Now, I'll totally let you continue your operations but you have to let me finish mine. This is important."

"I guess we'll be salvaging you guys too then."

The pirates cut the line.

"That happened." Rudy sighed. "Okay, familiarize me with the weapons because we're going to be in it."

"Analysis of the enemy vessel indicates that they are not as well equipped as ours. Their shields are enhanced consumer grade, meaning a few well placed blasts will take them down." Arak brought something up on the scanner. "Furthermore, they are *not* equipped with the continuous cannon that the other pirates were so we should be safe from retaliation."

"Weapons?" Rudy prompted.

"I've brought them online," Arak said. "Your triggers are on the flight wheel. Targeting computer is also up and ready. Just avoid the largest debris in the conflict and we should come out okay."

Rudy checked the scanner and saw their opponent was merely two hundred kilometers away but they approached behind a veil of tightly packed rockets. *That's interesting. Let's try something*. He pulled up, putting their target reticle directly in the center of the barrier blocking their target and opened fire with pulse cannons.

The rocks were obliterated, opening a perfect view of the pirates as they barreled toward them. Their plan seemed to be get as close as possible and go above or below the barrier to get a sneak attack in. As they started to bank high for their shot, Rudy fired again, clipping the back of their ship.

It spun to the right then engaged engines and tried to put some distance between them. Rudy pursued, taking their six. He hadn't done any real dogfighting outside the simulator in a long time. His ships were designed for a totally different purpose but he got back into quickly enough. Unleashing another blast, he barely missed.

The pirates continued to fly erratically and it became clear they knew the area well. Rudy smacked into some pretty sizable rocks and Arak casually informed him what each blow did to the shields. The constant reminder of the descending percentages started to annoy him but he was too focused to say anything.

The pirates pulled around a particularly large piece of starship, what looked like the frame of an engine. As they did, Rudy slowed and prepared for them to pop out the other side. Instead, they sprouted from the top and spun, firing a full blast that directly hit the top of the alliance ship.

"Damn it!" Rudy pressed the throttle forward, gaining some momentum before initiating the thrusters and spinning around. Just as the pirates would've taken their six, he was flying backward and facing them. Firing missiles and cannons at the same time, the pirate couldn't pull up in time.

Their front took the full brunt of the damage and micro-explosions dotted the hull of their craft. Rudy slowed them down again, just a few dozen kilometers ahead of running into another chunk of ship. The pirate exploded, leaving behind little more than dust and sparking metal. *Phew. That was nuts.*

"Excellent flying, Mister Hale," Arak said. "Our destination is approximately twenty-thousand kilometers back the way we came. I'll give you an indicator to follow.

I'm glad he thought the flying was okay but I expected a few more moments of elation that we made it before we got right back to business. I guess that's not how kielans roll.

Rudy got them moving again, this time even more cautious and aware of their surroundings. He reported back to the Behemoth and let them know about the attack. Revente advised caution. *If I wasn't with the kielans, I'd tell him off about that. Thanks for the news flash, Group Commander. I never would've thought of that on my own.*

As they approached their destination, he realized they'd been flying for well over forty-five minutes. *That was the longest three-quarters of an hour of my life.*

"Very good," Clea said. "Arak, I'm taking two people with me over to the ship when we find it. Please use the scan data in lines thirty-six to forty-eight for signatures."

"Yes, ma'am." Arak did as instructed and put a marker on the screen. "If the readings are correct, the *Tempered Steel* is right over there. Less than a kilometer away."

"Take us over there, Rudy." Clea put on her helmet. "You should be able to land on the surface. The drift, according to our readings, was not too bad."

Now I'm landing on moving garbage. This is definitely my day to be tested.

Rudy again moved them slowly toward their destination. Here, so close to the wreckage they were after, rocks continually bounced off their shields, bumped out of the way as they progressed. A ship with less protective capacity would be suicidal to try for any of the salvage in this place.

When he saw the hulk of the *Tempered Steel*, his heart pounded hard in his chest. Seeing a capital ship dead in space filled him with awe and a sense of sadness. Many people died on that ship, their bodies likely still floating in the vacuum of space, mixed in amongst this debris surrounding them.

He shook it off and approached, turning the ship to find a suitable point to set down. Reporting back to the Behemoth, he let them know they'd found their target and were on a final approach for landing. Revente acknowledged but the tension in his voice said he was worried. *Now I feel like I should be more concerned*.

Rudy matched the drift of the vessel and brought them down on what used to be the hull near the engineering section. It was the largest part of the ship still intact and he hoped it was the one that Clea needed to perform her investigation. The other part was some three hundred meters away, tethered to this part by a series of wires and a single metal panel that refused to break.

"Good luck, Ma'am. I hope you find what you're looking for."

"Me too, Rudy," Clea replied. "We'll be back as soon as we can."

***

Clea and two of the technicians, a woman named Tria and a man, Derra, stood in the airlock just off the mess area. They each double checked their environmental suits, ensuring none of them missed anything. Their computers stated everything was secure and sealed but sensors could break so visual inspection was necessary.

As the doors opened, Clea fought back a sense of panic. She'd never done anything like this before. Her zero G training was for disasters on ships, not trudging around on the outside of them. They'd get into the corridors soon enough but before then, they had a one thousand meter walk to the first access point, a shattered hole where the ship took a blow.

"I'll lead the way," Clea said over the com, forcing herself to take the first step. An irrational fear of her magnetic boots failing made her nearly hyperventilate but as soon as she felt them secure to the hull, she calmed down a little. Her companions seemed much more at ease, pacing out behind her without hesitation.

The second part of traveling in open space came from the difficulty of fighting the magnetic boots. It was like walking in deep snow and by the time they were half way to the hull breach, Clea's legs ached. She risked a look down at her computer and she looked back up, a rock sailed by at an alarming rate, nearly striking her in the head.

"Be careful," she said to the others. "I don't know if you saw that, but if the debris is moving that fast, it could be very dangerous."

"Understood, Su-Anthar," Tria said. "We're almost there."

The majesty of open space had to be acknowledged. Looking out over the boneyard, Clea couldn't help but feel awe at the carnage she looked over. Years of conflict and history floated out there in what amount to the middle of nowhere. Every broken up ship held a story of some kind along with lives lost or altered.

They arrived at the breach and cast a light inside. The floor was intact but they would need to use a bit of thrust from their oxygen pack to get down there. Once within proximity of the deck, their boots would do the rest but jumping wouldn't do anything but make them float off. Clea double checked her understanding of the controls before attempting it.

The last thing I need is to throw myself into deep space because I had no idea what I was doing.

"I'll go first, Ma'am," Tria said, stepping off the edge and engaging her thrust. Clea watched as the young woman descended, bending her knees as she connected with the deck and backing away easily.

Derra went next, leaving Clea alone to contemplate the area. She glanced over her shoulder and gasped just as a large rock connected with her shoulder. The force of it made her magnetic boots disengage and she floated, rotating so she was staring down at the deck below. "Engage your thrusts!" Tria's voice filled her ear. "Do it now, Ma'am!"

Clea nearly hit the wrong button, the one she would've needed had she jumped and not been shoved. As she tapped it, she began to sail toward her companions. The speed was alarming. She engaged the thrust to slow herself down but it took both Tria and Derra catching her to prevent her from hitting the deck.

"You okay?" Derra asked.

Clea nodded. "Yes, I'll probably have a bruise from that rock...but I'll be fine. Thank you for the help."

"No problem." Tria gestured. "The scan data we pulled suggests we need to go this way."

Clea cast her light about the area and instantly felt a rush of nostalgia and sadness. *Yes, you're right. It's that way. I walked this hallway a thousand times when it was part of a functioning starship. This is how I got to work every shift. Seeing it in such a state makes my heart hurt.*

She'd loved her time on the *Tempered Steel*. Her commanding officer had been a fantastic teacher and mentor. Those around her did their jobs professionally and made each day a joy to work. They were all reassigned to different vessels after the incident and she only spoke to a few of them ever again.

"Let's go." Clea swallowed hard and started along the deck, moving with a purpose. Her light illuminated the way but in her mind's eye, it was brightly lit as the day she first boarded. This visit bolstered her memory but she wasn't sure that was a good thing. As it filled in gaps she didn't even realize she had, it made her miss the ship all the more.

I guess most people look back on fond memories with nostalgic regret. I just wish I would've had more time with them.

They rounded a corner and paused. The wall to their left was missing, open to space like a window at a luxury hotel allowing a view of something exotic. Far off, they could just barely see the Behemoth. *We really came a long way!* Considering how large the ship was, to see it so small gave Clea more respect for the speed of their ships and the overall vastness of space.

"We need to keep moving."

They pressed on, coming to a door jammed shut. Tria stepped forward and pressed a rod roughly the size of a screwdriver at the center where they would open. She tapped something and it began to vibrate, wiggling its way between the doors. Once it was fully wedged into place, she pulled hard to the side and the doors slid open easily.

"Is that new?" Clea asked.

"Yes, it pulses energy through the door if you can get it partially open. That simulates the same power which gets the mechanism moving. It's a search and rescue tool now."

I'm sure they were using those when they were looking for survivors back at the research facility. I need to keep up with the advances in technology of my own people.

Pressing through, they walked for another five minutes before arriving at Clea's work area, the tech lab. The door was gone, though not from the combat damage. Clea performed a scan and frowned. *Someone cut this out.* She exchanged a glance with Tria and Derra. "Are you two seeing this?"

Derra confirmed. "Yes, someone's been here already." They all stepped inside and further confirmed the bad news. The entire area had been attacked by scavengers, down to the seats being removed. Most of the computer panels had been taken as well and even some sections of floor were missing.

Damn it!

Clea moved over to her station without much hope but she had to know if her data was missing. Tools weren't necessary. As she drew closer, she could easily see through the wall where her storage devices would've been. Checking the rest of the stations proved out the same information: all of them were missing.

This trip was for nothing!

Clea slapped the wall in frustration and tapped her communicator back to Rudy. "Bad news. Scavengers have already been here and taken everything."

"Oh crap…" Rudy sighed. "Do you want me to inform the Behemoth?"

"I'll let them know now, but thank you." Clea changed the frequency and contacted the ship. Agatha responded and quickly transferred her over to Gray. "Scavengers took everything. The storage devices are gone, sir. I'm…I'm sorry."

"For what?" Gray asked. "We had to check. Besides, I wouldn't despair just yet. We've got some people on board who might be able to shed some light on the situation. Head back to the ship as soon as you can and maybe when you return, I'll have some better news to share. Gray out."

"Come on," Clea said. "It's time to go back."

***

Major Harrington Bean was brought down to the brig for another interrogation, this time with pirates operating openly in the sector. These guys surrendered after their two companions were destroyed but not all of them wanted to come peacefully. The marines had to dislodge them from their vessel by venting gas into the ship, which gave them all a nice nap.

The worst of the bunch remained in their cells but the one who claimed to be an engineer was brought to interrogation. He seemed the most amiable to conversation so they figured Harrington would be able to get something out of him. Apparently, the tech crew didn't find what they were looking for so hope fell to the pirates to give them an idea of where it may have ended up.

The idea made sense. How many places could pirates offload illegal merchandise? Few reputable vendors in the alliance would risk the consequences. Those who didn't care about their reputation or operated well outside the law were also not likely to be listed in any business directory. All they had to do was find them.

Harrington observed the man through the one way glass for a moment, surprised to find he was human. Once the Behemoth was on the verge of active service again, the alliance had merchant vessels arriving to deliver goods. These ships took on industrious humans as crew members and passengers. They encountered some of them as pirates at the mining facility.

I'm a little ashamed to know my people left the solar system to be crooks.

The man had stringy, brown hair that hung low over his forehead, obscuring blue eyes. He sported a thick beard and his clothes had seen better days. The black vest was frayed and his brown shirt had been patched in several locations. *So these guys either don't spend their money on personal upkeep or it's a hard life. Probably both.*

Harrington stepped into the room and closed the door, opting for a direct approach.

"My name's Harrington Bean and I'll cut to the chase. You and I both know I'm in here for information. If you'd like to give it to me, this whole situation will go a lot easier for you."

The pirate looked up at him, scowling. "I already told people I was willing to cooperate. You took out our base ship. That was our meal ticket. Without them, we're back to square one."

"Then good." Harrington sat down. "What's your name?"

"Jessy Wilkens."

"Thanks, Jessy. So let's talk about how you make your money."

"Mostly, we just salvage tech from the boneyard," Jessy said. "We estimate there's enough here to keep people for another few years at least. Then there's the competition. We occasionally engage with them and take what they got. Not the most honorable of professions but it gets us by."

"Off topic, but why did you attack the Behemoth? Did you guys not know it was a warship?"

"We knew but our weapon...it should've torn through the shields quicker. We underestimated that part."

"Okay then." Harrington shook his head. "So back to how you make your money. What do you do with the salvage? I need to know every place you sell it to."

Jessy looked uneasy, turning his head away. Harrington recognized the expression as one of regret. He didn't want to talk about this part and probably had good reason. His compatriots would not look kindly on the guy who snitched out their cash spots. However, this is what he'd promised so he had to come clean eventually.

"I mean...I want to help...I do...but telling you that..."

"Is what's going to keep you from life in prison," Harrington said. "If you don't recall the regulations in this sector, the alliance has stated any act of piracy is punishable by life in a maximum security, work facility. Mining most of the time. You're looking at twelve hour days in some pretty miserable environments until you *die*."

Jessy pursed his lips, getting anxious. "It's just...I mean, at least I get to live in that scenario."

"You're wondering what happens if you tell me?"

Jessy nodded.

"I'll make sure your sentence is much shorter. A year or two at the most in a non-work related environment. You can get some education, clean up your act and come out with a clean slate. Providing you don't rush back to pirating, you can still make a life for yourself. Does that sound better than dying in prison?"

"Yeah..." Jessy sighed. "But if I tell you, they'll find me later."

"I don't have any interest in shutting down operations," Harrington said. "I'm only in this to find a piece of equipment. It's a wild goose chase but one we're willing to pursue."

"You're not here to bust pirates?"

Harrington shook his head. "No, we're here for information. This sector has all but been written off by the alliance. They don't care about the tech you're taking but if they knew what we did, they'd be out here enforcing the law a lot harder. Now, give me the information I need. Every broker who buys your merchandise."

"It used to move around," Jessy said. "To different bases in different sectors. Abandoned research facilities on asteroids, tough planets, moons and even a few derelict capital ships."

"What do you mean by it?" Harrington asked. "Surely, there's more than one."

Jessy nodded. "Yeah, but they're too far away. The one we frequented for the last few years is close by and always made it easy to offload goods from our trips into the boneyard. They're on a planet now only a short jump away. They set down in an oasis in the middle of a desert so no one could just waltz in from the outside."

"Defenses?"

"Oh, they've got some early warning systems. This big ol' thing isn't going to hop in unnoticed, not close by at least. And they don't let just anybody in neither."

"Talk to me about how we're going to get in then. We need to check the shops...the junk dealers."

"Only a pirate would get through." Jessy shrugged.

"How would you like to go home then?"

Jessy scowled. "What do you mean?"

"I mean if we need a pirate to get through the defenses and land, it sounds like you're the right guy for the job."

Jessy sighed. "This is risky."

"But not for someone who wants to get their life back."

Jessy really contemplated the situation for a time and finally nodded. "I need something if I do it."

"What's that?"

"If I go to prison, I want a new identity. And some money waiting when I get out so I'm screwed." Jessy looked into Harrington's eyes. "I need to disappear if I do this and you have to help me."

"We can do that. If you get us in there, then we'll hook you up with whatever you need to get straight. Do we have a deal?"

Jessy nodded. "We do." He gave them the coordinates for the pirate base. "That's the place we have to go. I can tell your navigator where this thing can hop into if it has to come along."

"Thank you," Harrington said, standing up. "I'm going to have the guards take you to a room to get cleaned up and changed. We'll probably need your help soon so get some rest. I have a feeling the next few days are going to be challenging."

Chapter 7

Gray, Adam and Clea sat in the briefing room. Harrington presented the information from the pirate and let them know the deal he made. He was dismissed when he finished and Adam turned to the others, looking grave. Gray figured he knew what the commander was about to say but he didn't interrupt.

"Clearly we can't keep this place a secret," Adam began. "These pirates attacked us immediately and had we not been an advanced warship, they would've taken us down. God knows how they treat crews but I'm thinking it's not five star."

"I agree," Clea said, "but we have to be cautious with the information. If we tell the alliance, they're going to want to come in immediately and roust the pirates. This base has eluded them for a long time. They're not about to let it get away again."

"Maybe we can give them the information and let them know about our operation," Gray said. "Our primary focus is finding the data. How're we going to get in there?"

"Impersonate the pirates," Clea said. "Major Bean considered it or he wouldn't have asked the prisoner to help. We have their vessel, we can just mimic it with the alliance shuttle. It's far more advanced and will give us an advantage if we have to get out of there in a hurry. Also, it isn't falling apart so it'll be safer to fly."

Gray grinned. "Yes, I saw their craft and it's not exactly in top condition." He turned to Adam. "What do you think?"

"Sounds dangerous but doable," Adam replied. "After all, we've seen how well Trojan horses worked in the past."

"Do you know what they barter with down there Clea? Are you going to be able to buy back the storage device if, through some miracle, you find it?"

"We've got the salvage on the pirate's vessel," Clea said. "We'll load that into our cargo hold and provide some of the tech we brought back from our trip. It's inconsequential to us but to junk dealers needing parts to repair rag tag ships, they'll be worth something."

"This plan's coming together." Gray hummed. "Okay, but we have to do something to that shuttle. It couldn't scream *alliance* more if we made it run a streamer."

"The insignias will be easy to remove," Clea added. "We just have to tarnish the hull a bit...take some of the gleam off of her. I think our engineers will have a few ideas."

"I'll leave you in charge of prepping the shuttle. Adam and I will figure out how we're going to get there undetected. You'll want us as backup. As long as we're in the system, we can monitor communications through your ship, using it like a satellite. Correct?"

Clea nodded. "Olly can set that up very easily and make it undetectable."

"Perfect. Sounds like we've all got a lot to do. Let's make it happen, folks."

***

The engineering team went at the alliance shuttle, tarnishing it up and giving it a lived in feel. They didn't want to remove all signs of the military from it, giving the crew some credibility at having stolen such a prize. Their work took over ten hours but when they finished, it looked more like the confiscated shuttle than the pristine, modern ship hiding beneath the surface.

Leonard received the coordinates and with the help of an updated database from their visit to the kielan world was able to map out the solar system they intended to visit. Olly helped him, showing him where long range early warning systems would be located to help them plan their approach.

In the end, they decided to jump in well outside the system, far enough away to avoid any possibility of detection. This meant the shuttle would not be accompanying them but rather disembarking from the Behemoth in the boneyard and heading in on their own. The ploy would help them sell their cover and with the salvage from the confiscated ship, they had cargo to sell.

Jessy worked closely with them on what would be expected. First, they had little protocol to worry about as pirates. No one really offered up respectful *sir* or *ma'am* and crews tended to be on a first name bases (or last name if the first was undesirable). He didn't get too in depth about the actual place they were visiting but let them know *it can be pretty rough*.

"What's that mean?" Adam asked at the briefing table. "I think our people need to know."

"Let's just say wearing weapons openly is a good idea. I've seen fights break out in the promenade plenty of times."

"I'm starting to formulate who should go," Adam said to Gray. "At least two marines."

Jessy nodded. "We do tend to keep a couple of hard types with us, ex military and such."

"Good," Gray replied. "Jessy will be going, of course."

"I'll guide them the best I can."

"Clea needs to go," Adam said. "She's going to be able to identify the parts we need and should be able to test them on the spot."

"Yes, I know." Gray hummed. "So two marines, Clea, at least one pilot, Jessy and I'm thinking an engineer. They might need someone to fix the thing."

"Then it'll have to be a kielan," Adam replied. "That Arak character seems to know the physical part of their ship the best. I'd recommend him."

"Sounds good to me," Gray stood. "Let's get Revente to pick a pilot."

Crews moved all the salvage over and packed it up. They also supplied the vessel, storing up just enough food to make it look like they'd been out in space for a while. Revente insisted on sending two pilots, as a contingency against something unthinkable. His rationale came as *if you lose one of those people and need a quick getaway, you're going to be in trouble.*

Meagan and Rudy were picked for the duty and arrived at the same time as Corporals Bobby Jenks and Dylan Walsh, the marines. They were dressed in civilian clothes, wearing their side arms. "Do you think we need guns?" Meagan asked.

"Yes," Jenks replied. "And we brought enough for everyone in our duffles. You'll want yours at all times according to the briefing."

Meagan wore dark jeans and a black sweater. As the marine handed her the pistol and holster, she checked it over. "Oh, lovely." She turned to Rudy. "When's the last time you fired one of these?"

"Shooting range with you," Rudy replied.

"It'll come back to you," Walsh said, "when someone starts firing at us."

"I like that you assume it's a foregone conclusion," Rudy pointed out.

"First off, when they send us, it's because they figure someone's going to do some shooting." Jenks ticked off on his fingers. "Second, we're rarely lucky enough to get in and out of a place *without* violence and finally, we're going into a den of criminals. God only knows what we're about to encounter."

"Fair points," Meagan muttered. "Come on, Rudy, familiarize me with these controls."

"It's more like what I fly than you do but they made it nimble enough." Rudy and Meagan disappeared into the ship and a moment later, Gray and Clea arrived. She too was dressed down, wearing cargo pants, a black vest and black sweater. Jenks and Walsh snapped to attention.

"At ease," Gray said. "You two might want to stow some of the discipline until you get back. You don't want to make such a mistake on the surface."

"We won't, sir." Jenks replied.

"Do you know these guys?" Gray asked Clea.

"Yes, sir. They were on the research facility mission with me." Clea offered them both a wave. "It's good to see you both again."

"You too, Clea," Jenks said. Walsh gave him an odd look. "What? I'm practicing being a pirate."

"Shouldn't you have said *ar* or something then?" Walsh asked.

"Okay, you two." Gray gestured for the ship. "I believe you're heading out in ten so you might want to stow your gear."

"Do you need a weapon, Miss An'Tufal?" Walsh asked.

"No, I'm carrying." Clea patted a holster on her side. "Thank you."

The marines boarded the vessel and Clea turned to Gray. "This is it."

"You don't have to do this," Gray said. "They are going to find anyone down there with storage devices and get them."

Clea shrugged. "I'm the only one who can find the exact thing we're looking for...if it's there. I have little hope at this point but I'm glad we have the chance to check."

"Be safe." Gray checked his chronometer. "We'll be out there if you need to signal us. Don't hesitate to call for help."

"We won't." Clea patted his shoulder. "I hope I make a decent pirate."

"You're probably too clean." Gray backed away. "Good luck."

"Thank you."

She boarded the ship and Gray headed back to the hangar control tower to watch them launch. Meagan requested clearance to depart and they hovered on the deck, turned and departed. Gray worried about this particular mission. Sending people into a blatantly dangerous location didn't set well with him, especially since it wasn't even a combat zone.

But they had preparations of their own to make and no time to waste. Gray headed back to the bridge to plot their own jump to be in a position where they could help their comrades should the need arise. He hoped Leonard figured out a good jump path to get them in undetected or most of this would be for nothing.

The last thing they needed to do was alert the pirates and spook them before their team located the data. If the criminals scattered to the wind, it would be months before they settled again. Any chance of finding that data would be lost. *We'll avoid that. I'm sure Olly and Leonard figured it out.*

***

Meagan let Rudy take the lead while she continued to familiarize herself with the controls. Watching the scans, she gave him a countdown of how far out they should get from the Behemoth before initiating the jump drive. Jessy provided the coordinates for where they should arrive, a brazen approach which suggested they belonged there.

"I've never initiated a jump myself," Rudy said. "Arak, are you going to be able to help?"

"It's very simple," Arak yelled from the back of the ship. "Input the coordinates and hit the glowing amber button. We'll arrive in short order."

"Is a jump any less pleasant on a smaller ship?" Meagan asked. "On the Behemoth it was hell the first time."

"Our technology and, from what I saw, yours now too, is much more sophisticated than the generation you're talking about. You'll barely notice the transition."

"I'll hold you to that," Jenks said, sitting on one of the bunks. Walsh sat across from him. "Should we strap in?"

Jessy stood nearby, holding a bulkhead as he watched through the windows with the pilots. "I never did," he muttered. "Not to say you guys shouldn't...if you have to."

"I'm not doing something a pirate won't," Walsh replied.

"Guess we're all daring it then, huh?" Jenks shook his head. "I wish I wasn't competitive."

Meagan turned to Rudy. "We're well out of range of the Behemoth and the course is ready. On your mark, I'll initiate the jump sequence."

Rudy nodded, leaned back in his seat and took a deep breath. "Go for it."

Meagan hit the button and the entire ship whined for half a second...then they were floating in a new sector, far away from the salvage and the Behemoth. Rudy engaged the engines and set their course for the nearby planet, their destination. Someone hailed them immediately, a frantic broadcast.

"Jessy?" Rudy asked. "What do I tell them?"

"Put them on speaker."

"Unidentified vessel, come in. This is landing control. Respond now or we will be forced to fire upon you. Come in!"

"Uh, hey there," Jessy said. "This is *The Fallen Star* coming in for a sell and supply. Over."

"*The Fallen Star?*" The guy sounded shocked. "We already have two of those here."

"We just claimed this ship and it sounded good," Jessy said. "How about we go with *Dark Star*?"

"Also have one already!"

"Damn! Um...*Wicked Night?*"

"That'll do." Landing control paused. "What's the clearance code?"

"Delta Charlie Tango Three," Jessy said.

"That's the one from last week!"

"C'mon, man! We've been out on salvage runs for a month! That's the code they gave me when we left. Are you really going to burn my ass over a code that only changed a few days ago?"

A pause…then, "fair point. Okay, you can land at bay eight. Take a careful approach from the north. The winds are picking up this afternoon."

"Thank you, control." Jessy shook his head. "I'm turning this over to my pilot now for any required updates on the weather."

"They're a bristly bunch," Meagan said.

"About as organized as a bunch of monkeys throwing a party, too," Jessy replied. "We're good now. I'll get everyone ready for the landing. There're a few things those soldier boys need to know if they want to make it on the surface."

After he left, Meagan smirked. "So what do you think? How's undercover work treating you?"

"Ask me after we've landed at the pirate base and wandered around with a bunch of criminals for a while," Rudy replied. "I hope this data's worth it. Hell, I hope we *find* it at all! This could end up being a *very* dangerous wild goose chase."

"Wow…" Meagan leaned forward to look out the window. The continent they were aiming toward appeared golden from the vast desert they were about to set down in. The rest looked green, possibly tropical. She ran a quick scan to get the surface conditions. Luckily, they'd miss the hottest part of the day by a couple hours. It would still be thirty-sex centigrade.

Lovely. We missed forty-seven by a couple hours. I'm glad we don't have to wander around in that. Still, it'll be a dry heat and dusty unless the oasis happens to be more humid than I'm guessing.

"Entering atmosphere," Rudy announced to the whole ship. It began to tremble, shaking as they descended toward the surface. Meagan grabbed the co-pilot controls in an effort to help him maintain a reasonable descent. The wheel vibrated violently in her hands, a good indication of just how much resistance pushed back at them.

Their nose began to glow as streams of air cooked around them. When they finally broke through, the wind pockets caught them and they compensated accordingly. *I haven't flown in atmo for a while. This should be fun.*

"You okay over there?" She asked Rudy.

"Yeah, but landing might be a challenge. I'm used to predictable, artificial gravity and this seems...I don't know...a little heavier than we're used to."

Meagan checked the scan. Sure enough, this planet enjoyed a slightly higher gravitational force than Earth. *Means we won't want to do much running around.* "You're right, but it's not much. Just don't compensate too much."

"I'm sure I'll be fine."

Meagan got on the com to the rest of the ship. "We're on our final descent, everyone. Please strap yourselves in and get ready for a landing. Shouldn't be long now. Temperature is hot as hell, gravity is heavier and we're going into a den of criminals so probably not the vacation destination you were hoping for."

***

The Behemoth jumped in shortly after the shuttle but they were quite a ways from the nearest early warning system. Even at full magnification, the pirate planet was barely more than a marble size. Gray watched the reports coming in, paying most attention to Olly's concerning the shuttle. They picked it up and it plunged toward the planet right on schedule.

Good luck, guys. Gray turned to Adam and showed him the information. The commander nodded and went back to his duties. They'd give the undercover crew five hours to accomplish their mission before informing the alliance about the location of the base. After that, they'd have to get out of there before a battleship showed up to put these thieves down.

"Sir?" Agatha turned in her seat to address him. "I'm picking up a message leaving the ship from tech lab seven."

Gray frowned, trying to think of who might be down there. He looked at Adam but the man shrugged. "What's it say, Ensign?"

"It's a warning..." Agatha's eyes widened. "Sir, someone is sending a message back to the kielan home world giving the coordinates of the planet!"

"What?" Gray stood. "Who?"

"It...it appears to be one of the kielans!"

"Damn it!"

"I'm not surprised," Adam said. "They have people to answer to as well. We can't expect them to keep quiet about something their people have been looking for. Especially since our reason for making them wait is all based on hope. We don't have actionable intel, sir. They're just taking advantage of a situation."

"Put me through to alliance command," Gray said. "Hurry."

"Um...but we're far away..."

"They figured it out," Gray interrupted. "Ask them how if you have to."

Agatha worked for a few moments, finally shaking her head. "I don't know precisely how they did it, but you're patched in through some kind of faster than light anomaly. The delay is only a few seconds!"

"That would've been nice of them to share," Adam muttered.

Gray ignored him, directing his comments to the kielans. "This is Captain Atwell of the Behemoth. Please note that we are conducting an undercover operation in this sector and cannot risk our people. Hold off on an attack until we let you know when. Believe us, we do not want these pirates running free but we *have* to get something from them first. Please respond."

The delay made Gray want to pace but he forced himself to stand still, finding some patience. When finally a voice piped through, he cursed under his breath. He anticipated the answer but he didn't like it regardless.

"Behemoth, this is alliance high command. Please note we will be preparing an offensive party which will take us approximately two hours. At that time, we will launch an all out attack on the pirate base. Have your operatives finish their business inside of three hours to avoid becoming casualties of this conflict. Alliance command out."

"Well, that's that," Adam said. "How're we going to tell them?"

Gray sat down, staring at the floor in thought. "First off, cut those kielans off from any external communications. No more chatting with anyone without permission. Second, Olly, Agatha...any ideas of how we can get them a message without tipping our hand?"

"The pirates have some fairly sophisticated scanners," Olly said. "Some of them are even military grade, likely salvaged from the boneyard. As long as they know how to use them, any transmission from off world will be intercepted."

"Not entirely true," Agatha said. "If we were to tap into their own systems, we could send the message through their communication net. To any logging programs, it would look like the com was sent internally and not from an outside force."

"But how do you get the signal to them without it catching you?" Olly asked.

"The shuttle communicated with them on the way down," Agatha said. "I've got the frequency logged. I can use that to cut through and send to them."

"How sure are you that you won't get caught?" Gray asked.

"Eighty percent, sir."

"Let's hold off and give them the warning closer to the deadline," Gray said. "That way if the pirates see the message, it won't matter. They won't have time to figure out we're out here."

Adam shook his head. "This is a much tighter timeline now."

"I know...but I don't think anyone thought this would be super easy. Now, it's just painfully hard. I'm sure they'll figure it out. The market down there can't be that big. Right?"

Chapter 8

Rudy set them down on bay eight as directed but he figured they should've called it a landing pad at best. The strip of stone was barely big enough for their ship and anyone performing maintenance might well end up standing in sand while working on the ship. Not the best conditions for starship repair.

"Leave the engine on low idle," Clea said. "Just in case we have to leave in a hurry."

"You anticipate much trouble?" Rudy asked.

"In this environment, I would not be surprised if we encounter some." Clea turned to the marines. "You two are with us but do keep a low profile. I'll do the talking with Jessy backing me up."

"Ma'am," Jenks said, stepping forward. He kept his voice low. "Are you sure we should bring him with us? How can we trust him?"

"He has quite the deal worked out with us so I don't think he's going to risk losing it in a hopeful attempt to find a new place to work," Clea turned to Jessy. "Are you?"

"No way." Jessy shook his head. "This life isn't really worth much. I'm happy to get out, seriously."

"Uh huh." Walsh glared at him suspiciously. "I don't really buy it but okay."

"Anyway," Clea said, "the four of us will go. The rest of you stay here and keep the ship prepped. Again, we'll probably want to get out in a hurry."

"We'll hold the fort down," Rudy said. "Good luck guys."

"I hope we won't need it," Jenks muttered, taking the lead. "See you when we get back."

***

Clea and Jessy led the way, stepping down the ramp in the back of the ship. A man met them at the end of the landing pad, dressed in greasy clothes which were covered in dust and sand. He smiled, revealing many missing teeth and his breath was rank even from thirty feet away.

"Do you need a resupply?"

"No, thank you," Clea said. "We're here to trade but we're fine on supplies."

"Maintenance? Refuel?"

Clea tried to walk by him but he moved in front of her. She scowled. "No, we're fine. Thank you."

"Anything at all? Women? Slaves? Contraband alliance vids?"

Clea sighed. "I'm about to lose my patience, sir and when I do," she gestured to Jenks, "he does something about it."

Jenks stepped forward, adopting a menacing expression. The man audibly gulped and nodded. "Understood, understood. But I like to offer right away. New blood might be a little desperate."

"I assure you we are not." Clea turned to Jessy. "Shall we?"

Jessy stood grinning at the scene and forced his expression to turn placid. He nodded quickly. "Absolutely. This way."

The entire base was built around what amounted to a lake. Palm trees towered over the buildings but had been cut back on the various landing pads surrounding the space. They stepped through a threshold which was little more than two metal planks held up by other, heavier objects. This offered some distinction between the area people congregated in and the space where ships were tended.

They passed by a number of storage containers of all sizes before seeing any people. A large crowd mingled about and the scent of cooking food filled the air. Jessy took the lead, plunging into the crowd like a diver might the sea. Clea followed in the small gap he left behind with the others remaining close behind.

"Keep your hands on your goods," Jessy said over his shoulder. "There're vultures in the food court."

"I'm sure," Clea muttered, placing a hand on her weapon to hold it in place. Her other objects were all well secured to her person and beneath her jacket. That might not matter to a particularly proficient thief though and paranoia began to tickle her neck. Just as she started to wonder whether she should start hugging herself to prevent losing something, they left the crowd and entered a clearing.

"Okay, shops are up ahead," Jessy said. "The most legit ones at least. There are a few less reputable ones but they rarely have the kind of exchange to buy what you're after. Those storage units can go for a decent amount."

"What do people do with them?" Walsh asked. "Delete them?"

"Yeah, clean 'em up and put them in their own ship typically."

Clea's heart throbbed in her chest. *I hope they didn't do that with ours. Lord, the data they might've casually wasted...*

A fist fight broke out not twenty feet from them. Two men began brawling, both at least a foot taller than Clea. The first slammed the other in the face and picked up a food tray. He began beating his victim over the back with it. Walsh took a step forward but Clea stopped him. The guy getting hit rallied and lunged forward, tackling his abuser to the ground.

They rolled around, exchanging blows over and over again. Blood splattered the ground, and one of the two went limp. No one attempted to break it up, not even when the victor casually reached down and snapped his opponent's neck. Clea stiffened as she witnessed the murder.

"That's seriously..." Walsh tensed beside her.

"It's not our fight," Clea warned. "Am I correct, Jessy?"

"Yeah, you don't want any. If you jump in now, then it'll look like some kind of event. Some other jerk will step up afterward and it'll just keep going."

"Where's security?" Jenks asked.

"Here? Ha! You two are our security. And anyone who has any sense brought their own too." Jessy shook his head. "You types...hilarious. Let's keep moving. Before someone notices your wide eyes and shock."

Clea hoped they might have two or three large junk dealers at the most. She felt her heart sink when they entered a massive bazaar with *dozens* of little shops lining the streets. Shouts called out wares and people desperately tried to attract customers, waving wares about like flags.

"How are we going to find what I'm looking for?" Clea asked Jessy. "This...could take forever."

"There are only a few dealers who would take on what you're talking about," Jessy replied. "I know which ones. Most of these types don't trade so much as sell. The guys I'm thinking of...they'll barter for goods. They've been doing this for a *long* time."

They continued along, looking over what amounted to the largest collection of stolen items Clea had ever seen. Clothes, luxury items, trinkets and more lined various stands, most of which were guarded by large men with guns. Clea wondered how often people tried to steal from these places, especially with 'personal security' keeping a close watch.

Jessy stopped in front of a stall, attracting the seller's attention. He came close and they spoke quietly for a moment. "You sure?" Jessy asked louder.

"I don't get that kind of techy stuff usually. It's too rare."

Jessy nodded. "Thanks." He gestured for them to move on.

Their next stop involved a man literally screaming at them to grab their attention. Jessy held up his hands as he approached. "Relax! We're coming."

"What can I sell you?" The man must've stood no taller than five foot two, his bald head covered in sweat. He looked about frantically, as if a sale might be the only way he survived the next half hour. "Circuit boards? Relays? Conduit cable? I've got it all, son. Just tell me what you need and I'll make it happen!"

"We're looking for alliance storage units," Jessy replied. "Just took a ship and need a few repairs."

The man's face dropped into such a state of depression, Clea wondered if he might commit suicide on the spot. He didn't look up for a time, finally letting out a massive sigh. It caused his jowls to tremble and when he met Jessy's eyes he shook his head. "I'm afraid I don't have any of those. But there are other…"

"That's all we need, bud." Jessy moved away. "Good luck."

"Wait!" The shrill cry made Clea look back at him. "Please! I've got other things to sell!"

Jenks leaned close to Walsh but Clea still overheard him say, "whack job alert."

"Seriously."

Only one left, Clea thought. *This does not bode well. Maybe there are other dealers Jessy doesn't know about. We'll have to scour these places if this doesn't work out.*

Their last planned stop took nearly thirty minutes to get to through all the crowds. When they arrived, they found a well appointed building that might've been a cargo bay at one time. Inside, a man sat behind a counter tinkering with a communication device. Clea looked around for the security guard but didn't see one. A sign said *Crandy's Shop*.

The place seemed much better off than any of the other stalls. Equipment hung from racks, neat and shining as if it were brand new. Crates of circuits and other small parts occupied the floor here and there. He even seemed to sell weapons, alliance military, which was probably the most illegal part of his operation.

No wonder my people want to find this place so badly.

"What can I do for you?" The man didn't look up from his tinkering. He just kept on working.

"You Crandy?" Jessy asked.

"I am."

"Nice to meet ya," Jessy said. "We're looking for storage units. Alliance make."

Crandy shook his head. "Sold out."

Clea stepped forward. "So you had some?"

"Yeah, sure did. Some crazy bastard actually figured out how to dislodge them without a wipe. Nice work and no idea how he did it considering he had no idea how to actually *read* them." Crandy shrugged. "Apparently, he didn't care anyway. Just wanted some money so he could fuel up and get back out there."

"But you sold them," Clea said. "To another spacer?"

"Most spacers can't afford a storage unit, not from me." Crandy looked up, squinting. "You don't seem like you need repairs."

"I'm looking for a specific set of them," Clea replied. "This place looks very organized. You don't happen to keep records of your items, do you?"

"If I did, it wouldn't matter to you." Crandy put his communicator down and rounded the corner. "Who are you people? What do you really want?"

"We need to find the storage devices you sold," Clea said. "It's vitally important."

"Treasure," Jessy interrupted. "Some alliance survey of a planet full of minerals just waiting for the taking. It's on their registry but we happen to know they haven't tapped it out yet. We're going for the retirement score."

"Oh, you are, huh?"

"You telling us you didn't look at the data?" Jessy asked.

"No, I didn't bother. Some of that stuff gets a guy killed just for knowing it."

"Please," Clea implored. "If you have information of where they might be, we need to know."

"What makes you think the owner hasn't already dug up the precious planet you're talking about?"

Jessy shook his head. "We don't necessarily. But the alliance lost the data before they could do anything about it and frankly, there'll be enough to share."

"With me?" Crandy smiled.

"Why not?" Jessy asked.

"You paint an intriguing picture but I think you're full of it. Even if you went out there and found this place, you ain't coming back to give it to me." Crandy shook his head. "I see no incentive for this deal."

Jenks stepped forward. "How about we don't hurt you?"

Crandy tapped a button and the door slammed shut. Turrets popped down from the corners and aimed in their direction. "You were saying?"

"Just a...hypothetical question..." Jenks held his hands up and stepped back. Walsh whacked him on the arm.

"Anyway," Clea moved over to him. "What will it take to convince you to help us, Crandy? We've got a ship full of scrap. You give us the information and it's yours. Everything we took in exchange for a lead on where to go next."

"How much do you have?"

Clea brought out her computer and showed him the sum. His eyes widened but only for a moment. Still, he gave away a tell. He wanted what they had. That was a good sign. She could work with that. She hoped.

"I don't know." Crandy scratched his head. "This sounds pretty dangerous for me. I mean, you guys are a pretty rough looking crew, coming in and threatening a shop keep like myself. If I send you out there and something happens, it might screw up business for me. And I'm doing fine without your scrap."

An alarm went off overhead.

"What's that?" Jenks asked. "I stood down, man!"

"It's not you, idiot." Crandy rushed around his counter and stared at a screen. "Oh my God...it's alliance! An alliance battleship just hopped into the sector!"

***

Gray read the standard reports from the bridge of the Behemoth, waiting as patiently as possible to get word from the folks on the planet. They were still well out of the range of the early warning technology and didn't intend to get involved unless they absolutely had to. He settled into a routine for over an hour before Olly shouted, making him jump.

"Captain! We've got a problem!"

"Jesus, Olly," Redding grumbled. "What's wrong with you?"

"Two alliance warships just jumped into the sector! They're launching fighters!"

"What?" Adam stood up and stared at the screen. "Whoa...that's...intense. I thought they gave us more time."

"They did." Gray scowled. "I guess they're early. Agatha, get them on the line."

"On screen, sir."

A kielan appeared with blond-white hair and jade green eyes. She looked impassively at Gray, allowing him to make the greeting.

"This is Captain Atwell of the Behemoth," Gray said. "We spoke to your command. What's the meaning of this? We were told we had more time before you arrived."

"I'm Captain In'Wa of the *White Light*. Plans change, I'm afraid. We were battle ready and did not want to allow these vermin to escape again."

"But we're looking for something vitally important down there," Gray replied. "We needed more time."

"Anything you need will be confiscated and you can go through it yourselves if you'd like. However, we're going to take this planet today and hold it. I do expect you to help, as members of the alliance."

"Well, hold on a second. You might want to know about a special weapon they have." Gray scowled. "They hit us with it and nearly took our shields out. That was *one* pirate. If they have more of those, you'll want to be cautious."

"Understood, Behemoth. Thank you for the warning."

"She cut the line, sir," Agatha announced, "but their com officer is setting up lines to our various departments to coordinate the attack."

Gray sighed. "Well, we don't have to be sneaky about informing our folks now..."

"I'm sure they know already," Adam said. "What do you think they're going to do?"

"Hopefully stay alive," Gray said. "Redding, microjump us into the action. Olly, get the readings up from the time we were hit with that laser. I'd like a little warning this time before they unleash it. Let's engage these pirates and help our new allies. Wouldn't want to start off on the wrong foot."

***

"What're we going to do?" Jessy turned to Clea. "This is going to get bad fast."

Jenks and Walsh took a position by the closed door, their weapons drawn. Clea turned to Crandy. "I assume you have a contingency plan for this."

"Not really," Crandy grunted. "But this situation...I'm kind of ruined. Are you jerks genuine about this planet?"

Jessy nodded. "Of course we are, man! We want to retire."

"I can get us to the ships *and* show you the most likely place to find your device but I have a price." Crandy scowled. "You have to get me out of here and share the wealth."

"Really?" Jessy rolled his eyes. "You have no other way off this rock?"

"We thought we were safe here. I can blow this place up to prevent real jail time but I can't make a living on ashes. And that's assuming I don't get shot before capture." Crandy turned to Clea again. "You seem like the one in charge so get me out of here. I'll make it worth your while."

Clea considered his request for only a moment before making her decision. They needed his knowledge. "Okay, what do we do?"

"Go out the back to avoid the real panic. It still won't be easy an easy path but I can get us to the landing pads. I hope your ship's big enough for everyone." Crandy rushed over to a computer terminal and tapped away. He hit a button and a countdown started. A door in the back opened and he snatched a duffel bag. "Okay, we've got fifteen seconds to get out of here."

"What'll happen?" Jenks asked as they hurried out the back. "Did you blow it up?"

"Kind of. It's locked down and I've got the code to open it back up but if someone tampers...everything inside gets blown." Crandy shrugged. "At least there'll be a chance they leave it alone and I can get my stuff back."

Clea sighed. *I have to report that as soon as possible*. "Just lead the way," she said aloud. "Everyone keep your head's down. I don't want injuries."

Outside the sounds of panic were nearly deafening. People in the market were rioting. Guns went off and screams erupted here and there. Ships launched, ready to do battle with the invaders. Clea's com went off and it was Rudy contacting her with an urgent request. She clicked it on as they moved. "Clea here."

"Ma'am, the landing pads are going *insane* with the arrival of the alliance," Rudy said. "We're locking down the ship and kicking on the weapons just in case."

"Keep the ship safe," Clea said. "We're making our way back but it might take some time. Things are crazy out here. We'll keep in touch."

Jenks and Walsh took point, their weapons raised. Clea drew her own, watching their back the best she could. They departed from the shop and headed toward the landing pads but had to go around several of the shops, moving along the rear. Others came pouring out, running for their lives.

"Contact!" Jenks shouted, aiming his weapon and firing. An armed man dropped to the ground, blood oozing from a wound on his head.

"He's got company!" Walsh gestured for the others to take cover and fired, moving toward a building. Another person went down, their weapon thumping in the sand. Someone returned fire, bullets clanking against the walls of shops behind them. Clea crouched, peering around the corner at their opponents.

It seemed a crew of six decided to engage them. "What is the point of this?" She asked Jessy. "What're they doing?"

"Trying to earn a little extra on their way off the planet, I guess," Jessy said. "These kind of opportunistic bastards just love taking what doesn't belong to them, even if it means risking their own lives in the process."

Jenks fired again, hitting one of the guys in the leg. Walsh finished him off and laid down some suppressive fire. "Reloading," Jenks spoke calmly as he replaced his magazine. "We have to move!"

"Any other way to the landing pad?" Walsh asked Crandy. "Or do we have to finish these guys off?"

"They're in our way!" Crandy gestured. "If we have to go around, we might as well surrender. It'll take an hour!"

Walsh and Jenks exchanged glances. They shrugged and returned their attention to the action. Their opponents, the three remaining, continued firing, using the automatic setting on their rifles to great effect. Jenks pushed away and went around the building, toward the riot. Clea wanted to call out to him but they seemed to have some kind of plan.

"Slow down!" Walsh shouted out to their attackers. "We're interested in talking!"

"You're going down!" The reply came out harsh, full of fury. Clea didn't blame them. Three of their friends were dead.

"Come on, don't you see what's going on?" Walsh poked his gun around the corner and blind fired. "We can't fight amongst ourselves right now!"

"Just stick your head out so we can wrap this up!"

A gun fired several times, fast enough that Clea couldn't count. She peeked around the corner in time to see the three guys dancing as they were shot, falling to the ground in a heap. Jenks stepped out and waved at them to join him. "Let's go!"

Clea stood, grabbed Crandy and forced him to run with her as they passed by the bodies and kept moving. Walsh and Jenks went to arm themselves, the latter pausing for a moment as he observed the bodies. They gathered up the guns and handed Clea a rifle. Walsh gave her a severe look. "You might need this, ma'am."

"I hope not." Clea slung it over her shoulder. "But good thinking."

"If we would've known it would be a brawl to get out of here, we would've grabbed some of that guys guns."

They reached a section where they either needed to plunge into the water or take a right and risk the crowds. Clea watched as people struck each other, grabbed things from stands and aimed weapons at aggressors. The man they encountered earlier who had been so twitchy lie on the ground, bloody and broken shot and beaten to death.

Wow...this is insanity!

"How's the water?" Jenks asked.

"Filled with some kind of horrifying fish," Crandy said. "You don't want to go in there."

"Looks like we've got man eating crap on either direction," Walsh replied. "Looks like we're risking the people threat."

They led the way, shoving people aside as they moved. A man attacked Jenks and was rewarded with a punch to the throat and a well placed stomp to his ankle. Walsh ducked a wild swing and fired his weapon into the man's gut. As he fell back, another person shoved him away and jumped Clea.

She took a blow to the face and stumbled backward but recovered quickly, blocking another attack. As the man brought his fist back, she lashed out with a palm strike to his nose, shattering the cartilage. He cried out, blood splattering over his lip as he stumbled away, collapsing to the ground. Before Clea moved off, she watched two people trample him and he went still.

The riot only picked up as they drew closer to the landing pad. Rocks flew through the air and they walked over more than a few people. Jenks and Walsh used their weapons conservatively, putting each round to good use. Eventually, the throng of the crowd became too thick to fight and people just mashed together until they reached the various landing platforms.

Ships had been taking off the whole time and a battle raged above them, far into space. Clea reached up and tapped her com but when someone bumped her, she ended up really whacking her own head. It made her ear ring as the connection was established back to their ship.

"Rudy, how're things?" She had to shout to be heard. "We're almost there!"

"We've kept them back with our weapons so far, ma'am," Rudy replied. "There are people in the landing pad though so be advised. We're looking at ten people trying to take the ship."

"Thank you!" Clea tapped Jenks. "We've got ten people at the ship trying to take it!"

"Won't be a problem," Jenks replied. "When we get there, we'll deal with it."

The crowds thinned somewhat as many of them peeled off for the different vessels. Many might've actually belonged on them but Clea doubted it. Chances were good they were off to pillage, using any desperate method to get the hell off that rock before the alliance landed troops to capture them.

Getting into space won't help most of them, Clea thought. *They're going to encounter some pretty serious resistance.*

They moved off the promenade and approached the doorway leading to their ship. Jenks and Walsh unshouldered the rifles and checked them out. As they reloaded, they turned back to Clea. "We're going to clear this place but I'm going to have Rudy help us."

"How?"

Walsh grinned. "Don't ask. Just stay back."

Jenks got on the com. "Rudy, I need you to start shooting. Drive these pricks back toward us."

He paused a moment and rolled his eyes. "Of course I want you to hit them! Put them down if you can, man! This is serious!"

Clea swallowed hard. The thought of someone being hit by ship weaponry made her stomach turn. The damage caused by such a weapon would be catastrophic. Considering the possibility, there'd probably be nothing left. She watched, much as she didn't want to, out of both morbid curiosity and a desire to help if needed.

The marines prepared themselves, holding their weapons at the ready. "Go!" Walsh shouted.

The weapons from their ship began firing. People screamed and returned fire, rushing back toward the exit. As they approached, Jenks stepped forward first, firing controlled bursts into the different men. Walsh followed suit, laying into the opposite side of the room. Clea held her own weapon up, staring down the site just in case.

Jessy and Crandy watched the back and suddenly started freaking out. Clea spun in time to see a couple men hurrying toward them, raising their weapons. She fired four times, two for each, and put them down before they got their own shots off. Her heart raced. She'd wondered if she'd ever be in another ground situation like the research facility again.

Much as she'd done on that mission, she still didn't feel prepared for this one.

"Clear!" Walsh's shout made her jump and she looked back. Bodies were piled near the walls and the marines rushed in, double checking to ensure they didn't have any more company. "We're good! Get the ramp open so we can get the hell out of here, Rudy!"

The ramp dropped and Meagan appeared, holding a rifle and aiming back toward the exit. "Come on!" She shouted. "Let's go!"

Clea urged Crandy and Jessy to go ahead of her and she hustled backward, watching out for any more enemies.

And they came.

Meagan fired first. "Contact!"

Jenks hurried over and fired as well into a crowd intent on rushing them. The combined fire of three rifles held their attackers at bay but they shot back, bullets careening off the hull of the ship. Clea dropped low and hurried up the ramp and took cover, aiming her weapon just in case they were overrun.

Walsh boarded next followed by Jenks. As they climbed aboard, a bullet entered the vessel and slammed into the ceiling. "Closing!" Meagan shouted, hitting a button. The ramp lifted as another spray of ordinance scattered across the hull. "Rudy, launch but don't go into orbit yet!"

"Why not?" Rudy shouted back.

"I have to check some damage to ensure we won't all be sucked out of a hole the size of my pinky!"

Clea turned and looked, fearing she'd see daylight streaming through. However, the bullet was stopped by a heavy beam going down the middle of the ship. They weren't in any danger. *Thank goodness!*

The ship tilted, shook then launched, departing the doomed pirate camp. Rudy kept them low, flying over the oasis and into the desert. Meagan ran a diagnostic scan before Arak showed up to do the same. They concurred that there was no appreciable damage. They could break orbit.

Clea set her weapon on one of the beds and sat down, trying to catch her breath. Walsh slapped Jenks on the shoulder. "That's how you get it done!"

"No doubt," Jenks said, taking a seat. "I'm thirsty. Is anyone else thirsty?"

"Who are you people really?" Crandy asked, sitting beside Clea. "Those two don't act like any pirates I've ever seen. That was some coordinated military stuff. Tell me I'm wrong."

"They're ex military," Clea didn't have it in her to put much conviction into the lie. "Just like all of us."

"You left the military to seek fortune, huh?"

Clea shrugged. "Considering the pay, wouldn't you?"

Crandy accepted it, at least he seemed to as he moved off. Clea didn't care. He'd help them because he wanted in on the action. He lost everything in that attack. Now, they needed to escape the alliance vessels attacking the area and find what this guy had to show them. If they could get out of the system, they might just still locate the device.

But considering the fact they just tried twice with no luck, she was beginning to lose hope.

Chapter 9

The Behemoth jumped into the fray just as over a dozen large pirate ships flew out to meet them. They were the types of ships they met at the debris field, not huge with probably crews of thirty or less but Gray knew what they carried and he instantly became wary of the battle about to take place.

"Launch all fighters," Gray ordered. "I want to get on those things with as much pulse energy as we can muster."

"Yes, sir." Adam went about giving the order. The kielans did the same, launching their own crafts to meet the incoming threat.

Agatha turned, "the kielans are offering them a chance to surrender."

Gray nodded. "They won't take it but that's civil of them. Redding, are we in firing range?"

"Almost, sir. I'm targeting the closest vessel now for a full barrage."

"Excellent. Olly, get our shields up and be ready to report when they start to use their special weapon. I want to be ready to move if we have to."

"Microjump?" Adam asked.

"Yes, that's my thought." Gray checked something on his data pad. "Olly, organize it with the engineering room. Looks like we get to test our equipment today in ways that I didn't entirely anticipate."

"Sounds good, sir."

I hope it's up to it. This is going to be pretty nasty if it's not.

***

Squadron Leader Mick Tauren took the lead for Panther wing while Meagan was away. His and three other fighter wings charged out of the ship, fully aware of the dangers they were facing. The enemy they traditionally fought had quite the firepower but these pirates harbored a weapon all of them should be worried about.

Revente told them, "their beam weapon damaged the Behemoth's shields. Any longer of a sustained strike would've opened them up. We don't know if they can aim it at something as small as a fighter but assume the worst and stay safe."

Going into the battle with that warning made them all leery but some of the younger pilots scoffed. "We'll know if the pirates are targeting us and just evade. Go under them. Maybe we can identify the weapon and where it's located to get out of the way."

Mick figured the gun was primarily designed for capital ships and it was how they took down their larger prey. A dozen large ships and perhaps twenty shuttle sized vessels charged out to meet them. Their job was to focus on the smaller ones then harass the bigger while their base crafts took them down.

Another five wings from the two alliance ships met up with them and coordinated the assault. *I wish we would've had these numbers the last time we fought the real enemy.* He figured the battle couldn't last long with so much firepower. Why the pirates hadn't surrendered made no sense to him at all. They were clearly outmatched!

The first of the ships they faced started taking shots at his wing, totally random blasts from an overcharged pulse cannon. Mick called for evasive and they all dodged out of the way, taking their own pot shots in the process. When his weapons scored a direct hit and splashed off the shields, he realized why the pirates had so much confidence.

They might not have the numbers but their technology defied the state of their ships. In other words, those shields shouldn't have been able to stop a direct hit but they did. Such modifications might've been performed on all of them, granting an advantage against superior, military vessels.

"We're going to have to hit these guys with concentrated fire," Mick said. "Pair up and do what you can. I'm thinking missiles will definitely be our friends."

They spread out, going at different ships across the way. One of their opponents dashed toward them with a quick burst then started firing like crazy. Mick saw Panther Six take a hit but it wasn't fatal. His heart hammered for a moment as he asked for a status. "Shields held, sir. I'm okay."

"Let's watch that stuff, this the kind of random we don't normally contend with." Mick and his wing man Flight Lieutenant Shelly Brown, performed a serious of hard maneuvers, quick turns and climbs to come around behind their target. As they did, they both opened up, firing missiles and pulse blasts at the same time.

Mick's cockpit instantly warmed until he began to sweat and he pulled up when they pulled within a thirty kilometers of their target. The missiles scored direct hits, the computer showing that their shields dropped down to thirty percent. Their pulse blasts knocked them down even further. "Get that guy! He's almost there!"

The pirate spun around and tried to flee toward the planet and as he did, two alliance ships closed behind and hit him hard from the top. Mick caught a glance of the ship being torn in half before exploding. Their allies moved off to another battle and Mick regrouped with Panther for another fight.

"The capital ship's up to something!" Panther seven shouted. "Look!"

One of the larger pirate vessels approached the Behemoth and deliberately turned their nose to her. *What the hell are they up to?* He didn't have time to wonder for long. A blast skimmed his nose and he dove, redirecting so he and his wing could take on another of the smaller pirates.

Mick's computer went crazy, warning about some kind of debris. "Avoid that!" He shouted, pulling up but he saw one of the alliance vessels pull right through it. Whatever they dropped clung to the hull, going right through the shields. A moment later, they exploded, taking the fighter with them.

Wow! Mines? Really? "These guys are fighting dirty, everyone. Stay on your toes!"

The entire wing converged on that pirate, letting him have it in a concentrated fire. He still managed to get a couple shots off before being taken down, clipping Shelly's side. She lost control for a moment, spinning away before slowing and returning to formation. "Damage report?" Mick asked.

"Minimal. All systems are still green. Let's keep it up."

These guys have managed to hit two of us and destroy an alliance fighter. They're doing better than the enemy does sometimes. I can't even believe it.

But even as the thought entered his head, he realized he shouldn't underestimate them. Many of the pirates likely came from the ranks of the military and probably knew the tactics they faced. It was like fighting colleagues in one sense. Each of them had to have come from a friendly culture.

Mick took a blind shot to the engine. His power fluctuated twice before remaining steady. He checked his damage and saw that something got knocked loose in his generator. Someone would have to manually fix it on the hangar deck. *And if I jostle too much, I may loose power entirely*.

"First off, I'm okay for the moment but that hit damaged my power relay. It could come totally loose and I'll be useless. Second, who hit me? I want to return the favor before I have to go back to the Behemoth."

"We're on him, sir." Shelly and the others dove, screaming toward the enemy at full speed. More blasts flew past them as they each unleashed a missile, six projectiles hurtling down the pirate. As they connected, Mick checked his scan to see the shields were eliminated and massive hull breaches spread throughout the ship.

A couple pulse blasts from one of his wing knocked them out completely.

Other dogfights went on all around them. Ships diving and veering to avoid destruction. One of the capital ships fired its beam weapon at the alliance vessel, chewing at its shields like an entire colony of termites. A human ship, he thought maybe from Tiger wing, went down and a couple more alliance fighters were destroyed as well.

The pirates gave far better than Mick would've anticipated. His power pulsed again and he determined to make his way back to the Behemoth. "I'll be useless to you guys if I don't get this fixed. Hopefully, they can plug it in and get me back out here in a flash."

"I'll cover you," Shelly said. "The rest of you form up and concentrate on the next vessel. We'll be right back."

Mick pushed it, heading for the Behemoth as fast as he could manage. The enemy vessel that faced them began to fire their beam weapon. He winced...then his stomach dropped when the Behemoth microjumped away. *Oh crap...where'd they go?* It took his scanners a moment to see he had another five thousand kilometers to go.

Better adjust course. I hope they're ready to take us on. Pretty bold move. Good job, guys. I only wish I'd been on board before you did it.

***

Olly tapped his screen. "The fighters are doing okay but those pirates are pretty dangerous. The tactics are...nothing short of dirty."

"I figured as much," Gray said. "Leonard, do you have a course for a microjump?"

"Yes, sir. It's plotted and laid in. We just have to initiate it."

"Perfect."

One of the larger ships turned to face them, giving them their nose. Adam spoke up, addressing Redding, "give that bastard everything you've got."

"Yes, sir." Redding fired, letting all the cannons hit the pirate at once. Their shields were decimated but it didn't quite destroy them. "We're on recharge. Ten seconds."

"How're the alliance ships doing?" Gray asked. "Are they still with us?"

"Yes, sir," Olly replied. "They've taken down one of the larger enemy...it seems the pirate tried to ram them."

Adam shook his head. "What's the deal with ramming? That shouldn't even be a tactic."

"Effective if you have a death wish," Gray muttered. "Redding, fire."

She let loose another torrent just as the enemy fired their beam weapon. "Direct hit to us!" Olly shouted. "Shields already at sixty percent!"

"Jump," Gray ordered. "Now!"

Redding hit the button and the ship winked out. Olly hoped to God the engineers truly fixed the jump module the way they said. As they reappeared, without incident or negative sensation, he decided they needed a fruit basket. *Or at least a drink. I'm totally buying them a drink.*

"We've repositioned," Redding reported. She sounded shaken though. Clearly she expected worse from the jump. "Redirecting our fire to eliminate our target."

As they fired again, the enemy vessel cracked and listed before turning into an orange ball. *One more down.* Olly checked the scanner. There were nine more large vessels combat ready. He analyzed each and found that they were in various stages of damage. Apparently, they were taking quite the beating as well.

Agatha spoke up, "sir, Panther two has contacted hangar control for permission to land for hot maintenance. He's asking we don't microjump for the next few minutes."

"Tell him not to worry, we've got other problems," Gray said. "Agatha, can you reach Clea's party?"

"Attempting to now, sir."

"Do you think they're okay?" Adam asked.

"I guess it depends on what the conditions are like down there," Gray said. "It could be pretty bad. If it's completely lawless then no one's trying to maintain order while the military attacks their base. Get us into position for another strike on one of those ships, Redding. I want this wrapped up."

***

"Miss An'Tufal?" Rudy called from the cockpit. "Can you come here please?"

Clea hurried over to him and leaned close. "What is it?"

"I'm getting a message from the Behemoth on a coded channel. We've got the coordinates from that Crandy guy and are ready to jump. What do you want to do?"

Clea took a headset and put it on, sitting in the passenger seat behind Meagan. "Patch me through to Gray, please."

Gray's voice crackled in her ear. "What's going on? Did you make it?"

"We're safe," Clea said. "But we're pursuing this further. A junk dealer knew who might've bought the data storage devices and we're going to get them."

"Wait, you're jumping out?" Gray hummed. "I don't think that's a good idea, Clea. Come back to the ship and we'll go together."

"If we do that, we risk losing the cooperation of our passenger."

"You took the junk dealer with you?" Gray sighed. "Clea, this isn't part of the plan. You don't know what you could be jumping into."

"We're sending you the coordinates so you can meet us there," Clea replied. "We'll scope it out and see what's going on, buy you some time to arrive. If it's nothing, then we can just board the Behemoth and go home but if it's something…"

"Be careful, Clea. With everyone on board, be careful."

"Of course, sir. Clea out." She put the headset away. "Let's get far enough away to jump out of here without attracting attention."

"Plenty of people who evacuated are doing the same thing," Meagan said.

Clea looked out the window and witnessed several ships jumping out all around them. *That's what the fight is out there. A chance for all these folks to get away. We got to nestle ourselves amongst those who needed to flee. Fantastic news for us, I suppose. Though I'm guessing the guys who wanted to take the ship would've used it to fight.*

The pirates had a strange loyalty if they were willing to risk their lives to let their dealers and services escape. She wondered how many of them would try to flee the alliance once the majority of the planet escaped. How many *would* get away? Considering the firepower being brought against them, she doubted much. Even with their dirty tactics, they weren't a match for three capital ships and all the fighters they had at their disposal.

"Hey," Meagan spoke quietly. "Panther wing's out there somewhere. I just saw a ping from Mick. He took some damage."

"I'm sure he's okay," Rudy replied. Clea heard the tension in his voice. She knew he'd lost a man in their last mission and was still trying to cope with it. "He's a tough guy."

"I know," Meagan said. "I wish I was out there with them."

"This is important," Clea replied. She put her hand on the pilot's shoulder. "Believe me, if this works out, we're going to change things for the better. Not just an engagement either but the whole war. You'll see."

"I hope so," Meagan said. "I'd hate for us to be fighting pirates for nothing."

"Any unnecessary combat is regrettable," Clea said. "Don't worry. I'll explain more when we get there. If we're ready for the jump, let's get strapped in to make it happen. Thank you both for your help. Let's see this through now."

***

Gray rubbed his eyes after the conversation with Clea. *This has gotten out of hand*. They shouldn't be on a wild goose chase throughout the sector. He hadn't anticipated this investigation taking an onion turn. Layers annoyed him. He figured they would either find the device or nothing on the pirate world, not another location.

And what happens if she finds another trail to follow? The obsession with this data became clear to him though kielans handled such things differently than humans. The signs were far less overt. She needed to follow this to the end but it might not entirely be the best thing for the military or the people with her.

"We've taken another one down." Redding's voice interrupted Gray's thinking and he looked up. "They were about to fire that weapon of theirs again."

Gray nodded. "How many are left, Olly?"

"Seven." Olly hummed. "Sir, I think they're preparing to retreat."

Adam sighed. "They bought the time they needed."

"Agatha, let the kielan ships know." Gray rubbed his chin. "I have a bad feeling we're going to be on clean up here."

"Was that Clea on your personal com?" Adam asked.

Gray nodded.

"I'm guessing her message wasn't something you wanted to hear."

"Not particularly." Gray looked at his personal message queue. A set of coordinates sat at the top. He sent them over to the navigation console. "Leonard, I sent you something I need researched. Get all the information you can on the sector *quietly*. I don't want our friends to find out about that too."

"Yes, sir." Leonard looked back at him. "I'll compile a report as soon as possible."

"Thank you." Gray turned to Adam. "Let's help our allies wrap this up. I'm afraid they didn't do a very good job of keeping this place locked down."

"I'm not entirely surprised. The pirates were fighting dirty *and* they didn't have any regard for their own lives. We've seen what a lack of self preservation does in a battle."

"Two ships escaped," Olly said. "Three others have been destroyed and two have been disabled. The kielans are moving in for a capture. The smaller vessels have also been wrangled up. Looks like this fight's over. Kielan troop carriers are descending to the planet."

"Whoever they find down there's going to be frantic," Gray said. "And probably not very cooperative. Let's offer up some support for that. Agatha, ask if they'd like any of our marines to accompany them to the surface. We need to expedite this situation as quickly as possible so we can get back to our business."

Before it's too late, Gray thought. *I hope our people are ready for whatever they're about to encounter.*

***

Mick landed and didn't even make a motion to get out of his fighter. Three people rushed forward, ran the fastest diagnostic he'd ever seen and opened the maintenance panel. His computer showed their progress and when they reattached the cable, all lights turned green. One of the techs moved over to see him through the cockpit, offering a thumb's up as he spoke.

"You're good to go! Shields are nominal and all systems are up! Good luck!"

The techs hustled away and Mick launched again, plunging back into space and toward his wing. He sent a ping to let them know he was back in the fight and gunned it, full throttle back into the action. As he flew closer, he saw one of the larger ships trying to gain a firing solution on Panther Four, Shelly.

Mick set the targeting computer to task but couldn't wait for it to get a lock. He manually aimed, firing his pulse cannons. A near miss but it caused the enemy to pull to the side, buying Shelly a little space. "Glad to see you, Mick! Thanks for the assist."

"No problem," Mick replied. "This might help a little more."

He fired his missiles the moment he got tone. Two of them dropped from his craft and raced forward, chasing his target. The pirate pulled away, disengaging from Shelly but it didn't help. The missiles continued to pursue him, striking the engines dead center. The shields flared then, the craft began to flip far too fast.

Mick imagined the inertial dampeners couldn't keep up with such a maneuver and as the ship just kept on going, he figured the people inside must be dead. They didn't even try to recover but their shields began to recharge even as they drifted off, away from the battle.

"Form up on me," Mick ordered. "Let's see who's left."

"All wings," Revente's voice filled the channel. "We are receiving surrender notifications from various pirates in the area. Stand down and hold your distance. I do not put a trick past these people and I won't risk any pilots on deceit. Let the capital ships take care of this part and good work."

"Wow," Shelly said. "You flew all the way back out here and *still* managed to take one out before the fight ended."

"Lucky I guess," Mick grumbled. "I'm surprised. These guys seemed ready to fight to the death. What happened?"

"Looks like a bunch of ships escaped from the surface," Kelly, Panther Eight, replied. "I've got a feed from the Behemoth. A ton of vessels fled the sector during the engagement. They're sending marines down to see who's left."

"There you go." Mick shook his head. They'd been distracted. His estimation of the pirates changed dramatically. If they were capable of sacrificing themselves for others, maybe they weren't the mercenary scum he'd thought them to be. He figured they were the *every man for themselves* type but the valor displayed said otherwise.

Some of them even surrendered. Incredible.

"We're on security detail," Mick said. "Let's keep our formation tight and wait for orders, folks. I guess this fight's all over."

Chapter 10

Clea strapped herself in, anticipating their jump. Meagan clicked her tongue. "Kielan capital ships sent out a message warning all ships to remain in the sector. Apparently, they're locking everyone down and no one's to leave. Imagine that? Authorities wanting to arrest criminals. What a galaxy we live in."

"Hush," Rudy muttered. "I'm about to do the scariest thing I've ever done."

"Admit you can't fly?" Meagan asked.

"You're incredibly funny. Definitely worthy of taking stage."

Clea recognized the banter as a defense mechanism. They were afraid of jumping in a small craft. She'd done it before so the prospect didn't bother her nearly as much. But listening to the tension in their voices, it gave her pause to think about it. Maybe she *shouldn't* have been as comfortable. Then again, the technology was tried and true. She had no reason to worry...

"Her we go." Rudy hit the button and the ship vibrated. A moment later, they were in another place, far from the pirate planet. "Whoa! That was...that was..."

"Really smooth," Meagan said. "Easy even."

"Incredible. I wonder if they could install one on the bombers." Rudy shook his head. "Talk about a tactical advantage."

"Full stop," Clea ordered. She took her safety belts off. "I want to talk to our passenger before we go any further. We have no idea what we're about to walk into."

Moving back to the cargo area, she found Crandy admiring the scrap they had aboard. "You guys weren't kidding. You've got quite the haul."

"Yes, it's a lot." Clea folded her arms over her chest. "Tell me where we've gone. Who are we meeting?"

"He's a collector," Crandy said. "A crazy old bastard from the early days of the war. He used to work for the government designing weapons. At some point, he got tired of it and just left. He's been buying up tech from battles all over the galaxy since then. If your storage device is still intact and not wiped, he's got it."

Clea nodded. "His name?"

"Durant Vi'Puren."

Clea instantly knew the man. He was a legend in the scientific and technology community. His designs helped bolster their shield technology, enhanced their weapons and provided better protection for ground troops. Small arms and scanning devices also benefited from his genius.

She thought he'd passed away several years ago. When he disappeared, most thought he just wanted to retire but there was always a cloud around his departure. No one could find any information on it and Durant stopped publishing articles or theories. He'd effectively disappeared.

So he went off to conduct his own research. Interesting. But why? What would've led him to leave us in the middle of the war?

Clea turned to her data pad and brought up the man's public record. Her eyes widened when she saw how old he should be: seventy-three. He'd seen a lot of conflict, four decades of fighting. And more importantly, he knew what it was like *before* the enemy declared war on them. That made quite the difference.

No wonder he wanted to get away from it all.

"Have you ever seen this man?" Clea asked Crandy.

"Yes, a couple of times. Fancy bastard stuck out on our little retreats but he always brought plenty for all. That beam weapon the pirates use? He made that."

Well, that's a treasonous act. Really, Durant? Why arm criminals with something so potent? That's reckless to say the least.

"I see." Clea shook her head. "Then we need to be cautious going toward his home. I have a feeling it will be well defended."

"That's a guarantee," Crandy said. "Well…at least, I'd think so."

Clea returned to the cockpit, passing by Jessy on her way. He was complaining to the marines about how dangerous the situation was and how he shouldn't have come. Jenks told him to shut up before she got out of earshot. The man was right. Their trip went from mildly dangerous to extremely.

"I need to perform some scans." Clea sat at one of the terminals behind them and began working on the computer. "This should only take a moment to find the system we want then I need to hail the person living there to ensure we're not destroyed the moment we hit atmosphere."

"I'd like to avoid that," Rudy said. "Just...you know, if we're voting."

Clea smirked. "I'll let you know when this becomes a democracy, Mister Hale." She went about checking the solar system, running their long range scanners for any habitable space bodies. There were six planets orbiting a relatively old star. Of them, one was capable of easily supporting life without alteration and another might've been viable with proper terraforming.

Various moons might hold bases which could easily sustain life but the expense of doing so should've been beyond a single person. Clea wasn't sure how of the resources Durant might command though so she needed to find any technology in the area and map it out. From there, she figured she'd pinpoint a primary location where inhabitants might dwell.

The first thing that popped up made her groan. A satellite on the edge of the sector, just on the border before departing. It had scanned them and she didn't know until she took an energy reading from it. *Okay, Durant knows we're out here. Now, where is he?* She started a long term scan and got on the ship wide com.

"Crandy, please report to the bridge."

Crandy arrived a moment later, leaning in to look at her. "What?"

"How did you know this man was out here?"

"He's had things delivered to him before," Crandy replied. "Guys bringing him some of the bigger stuff he bought. Always been that way."

"And it didn't seem to matter to you that there's an early warning system in place?"

Crandy shrugged. "I thought we were coming to talk."

Clea sighed and hit the com channel, opening it wide. "Mister Vi'Puren, this is Clea An'Tufal. We're not here in a hostile capacity. We just need to talk. Please respond."

They were met with silence. Clea glared at Crandy and tried again. "We may have information that you want concerning the enemy and, quite honestly, I think you might have something we need as well. Please respond."

This time, the speakers crackled as if someone did *acknowledge* their message but no reply came. Clea considered what exactly she might say to pique the man's curiosity. What did he need or want that might bring him to the line? Honestly, she'd be bluffing with most anything she had to offer unless he hadn't seen the data on the drive they were after.

Maybe that'll be the ticket.

"Sir, we're looking for something of great value on a storage drive you may have procured," Clea tried. "If you'll simply let us talk, I'm certain we can't work something out. Please, we're rather desperate."

This time, a response came immediately. "I've been listening to you, Miss An'Tufal. I knew your father."

Clea's heart hammered in her chest.

"If you've turned to piracy, he won't exactly be proud."

"I assure you there's a reason for everything," Clea replied. "Can you please direct us where to land? I would like to speak to you in person."

"Just know that if you're here for nefarious reasons, I have defenses that will liquify you. I don't tolerate hostility."

"And we're not bringing any, I assure you." Clea clenched her fist. "Please...you have to trust us."

A long pause made Clea worry he'd cut the line. She was about to speak up when something in the back of her mind to remain patient. *Let the man think it through. He's become a reclusive hermit so he's not exactly used to guests who are there to talk. Selling things is a far cry from visiting.*

While she waited, she brought up Durant's file and looked over his accolades again. He'd won every science award the kielan people had to offer. Prior to the war, he'd been responsible for making space travel safer through environmental shield improvements and he also enhanced the artificial gravity, making it more pleasant to live in.

When the war started, he shifted his focus to arms, a point which must've bothered him considering his previous work. Putting his genius to destruction went against some of the awards he won, the things which showed his dedication to peaceful expansion. Due to patriotic zeal, no one called him out for the shift in direction, not in the beginning.

Clea found an article about a protest group in the last years of his government work who called him a hypocrite. Some grew so tired of the fighting and losing family members that all the patriotism in the universe couldn't assuage their frustration. They lashed out at anyone they perceived as having to do with prolonging the conflict.

Some even went so far as to say Durant was war profiteering. He never addressed any of these allegations. He just left and Clea couldn't necessarily blame him. He'd given his entire life to the kielan people, devoted it to improvements and defense only to eventually be lumped into the problem.

Why stay?

"Alright, Miss An'Tufal. I've decided to trust you. Remember my warning. I'm sending you the coordinates to where you can land." The line went dead just after a series of numbers appeared on her console.

Clea sent them to the pilot station. "Please make course for that location," she said. "We just got clearance to land."

"Do we want to?" Meagan asked. "It sounded like you really had to work to get that permission."

"This is our destination, Miss Pointer," Clea replied. "We need to see where this path ends."

"I hope it's not on another planet," Rudy said. "Because I'm not sure our mission parameters are going to extend beyond this visit."

"I agree." Clea nodded. "I'll be in the back briefing the others."

She left the bridge and found Jessy, Arak, the marines and Crandy all gathered in the mess area. The table and chairs were secure to the deck and they were sitting around, sipping from cups. She paused at the door before launching into where they were about to land and how she expected everyone to remain on their absolute best behavior.

"This guy's a bit of a nutter," Crandy said. "So don't push him. He's old, eccentric and has lived alone for a *very* long time."

"A good warning," Clea agreed. "We don't know how much he's changed since his work with us so many years ago. I'm quite certain whatever he's been able to build out here all alone will be spectacular. I'll be playing to his ego somewhat, giving him the credit he probably feels he deserves. We need that storage device or at least what's on it. I'll do the majority of the talking."

"Suits me," Jenks said. "I've never been good at chatting it up with scientists."

"You're terrible at talking to anyone," Walsh replied. "What makes scientists special?"

"They're techier than everyone else. I can't really follow. I know how to use my data pad but other than that, I'm not a deep dive kinda guy. Not on machinery at least."

"I beg to differ," Walsh muttered.

"What's that mean?" Arak asked.

"You don't want to know," Clea interrupted. "Anyway, we'll be landing shortly so prepare yourselves. I'm fairly certain this is going to be an educational experience."

***

Hoffner's people were busy processing prisoners the Behemoth took onboard. Some of them weren't as ready to give up as the captains who commanded the ships and fights broke out immediately. At one point, they had to seal an entire ship and gas it to knock out the inhabitants then carry them out while wearing environmental suits.

Another set of pirates pretended to go easily and as they were being marched to the brig, they attacked the marines, trying to confiscate their weapons. Hoffner's men proved to be more than a match for them and they beat them down, killing one. As they got them to the cells, the captain of the pirates confessed that they were planning to commandeer the Behemoth.

Once their brig was full, they sent the rest on a shuttle to their allies. It took nearly two hours to get everything worked out. Then there was the surface mission. When they landed, the soldiers were met with a bunch of stranded, rioting pirates or their support staff, all desperate to leave the planet at any cost.

A few major firefights broke out with two marines getting injured and over a dozen dead or wounded on the pirate side of things. Once they realized the kielans and humans were there to arrest them, they gave up peacefully and allowed themselves to be transported back to the various ships for processing.

The kielans confiscated nearly three tons of total contraband cargo. Much of it had been stolen though some was legitimately salvaged. Unfortunately, no one had one or the other so the combination of goods put these people in dire straits. According to alliance law, being caught as they were, most looked at years of prison time.

They found a large cargo container registered to a man named Crandy. When the kielans tried to open it, the inside exploded, destroying everything inside and killing one of the men who picked the lock. All the evidence inside was incinerated, leaving nothing behind. They made a note to keep an eye out for him, especially since he was the only one who sabotaged his own stock.

He must be on one of the ships by now, Hoffner thought. *I'm sure they'll figure it out.*

He spoke with Marshall and discovered the captain was desperate to get moving, to follow their undercover crew to another sector. Word from the bridge was the marines should be ready to move if necessary. The captain had a hunch about what they'd find and wanted everyone on their toes.

Hoffner briefed his folks, putting them on alert. They still had some time before they'd be able to jump out of the system. The kielans wanted to make sure everyone was accounted for and the work they were there to perform was completed properly. Had they not shown up early, the Behemoth might've gotten their data and been able to go home.

Nice of them to screw us over. Hoffner couldn't help but be a little bitter. Their next adventure put his guys directly in danger and that didn't set well with him. Especially when the threat was completely unknown. *I guess we'll see how bad it is soon enough.*

He went back to helping coordinate prisoners and gathering IDs. Security people would be busy through the jump and beyond. None of them would have time to worry about where they were going and in a way, that suited Hoffner. His folks didn't need time to think when they were on the verge of a potential fight.

***

Meagan took control from Rudy so he could take a moment to stretch. She approached the second planet, the one closest to Earth's atmosphere according to Clea. It looked a lot like home but the continents were all wrong. The cloud coverage reminded her of the first time she went into space on her own. She looked back over her shoulder and gasped at the majesty.

Even all these years later, she still felt a sense of awe when approaching a world. So much went on down there and to see it all at once gave her quite the thrill. It was such a privilege to gain perspective on how small a big world really was. Though there may not be a lot of civilization where they were going, life had to be flourishing there for it to be so blue and green.

Rudy returned before they broke atmosphere and took his seat, yawning. "I think I need a couple days of sleep to recover after this."

"Probably," Meagan said. "You've always been lazy."

"Nice." Rudy shook his head. He got on the com. "Um…control, this is…" He muted the line and turned to Meagan. "What did that maniac call the ship?"

"*Wicked Night*."

"Thanks." He unmuted. "This is the *Wicked Night* requesting clearance to land."

"Yes, yes," an irritable voice replied. "Just land already! You have the coordinates. You don't need to keep asking for it like an errant child desperate for a sweet."

The line went dead and Rudy smirked. "He's salty."

"Yeah, not entirely social, huh?" Meagan maintained control of the ship as they broke atmosphere and began their descent. She had gotten the hang of the craft throughout the last hour as they approached and bringing it down felt fairly natural, despite most of her time being spent behind the controls of a fighter.

As they broke the cloud coverage, they found themselves flying over a vast forest that stretched on as far as the eye could see. Meagan's eyes widened as she considered the implications of what she saw. This place was a wealth of resources, totally untouched by any culture. It seemed impossible.

"You thinking…"

Rudy nodded. "I am. This is pristine. I can't believe it."

"I wonder how he's kept it safe." Meagan checked her scanner. "There's plenty of water and life down there too. Mammals and fish at least...and minerals. Wow, I'm picking up a lot of heavy metals too. The types we use for building ships."

"Incredible. Maybe that's why he set up shop here. To use the resources for his own work."

"One guy couldn't mine all that," Meagan said. "It's impossible. He'd never get enough and process it to make any difference."

"I wouldn't put it past him," Rudy replied. "Look over there."

He directed her attention to a brilliant silver spire that stretched up a good six stories. A complex, easily large enough for a small factory, spread out near a rocky outcropping with a waterfall to the left and the forest encroaching on the borders in front of it. Meagan saw the landing pad and redirected for it but she couldn't help but stare at the construction.

"This place is amazing. How did he get it here?"

"Prefab housing maybe," Rudy replied. "It has to be. I wonder how long he's lived here...and added on to this place."

"Must've been years. This is practically a small town. Hell, it's bigger than where Mick grew up, I can assure you of that."

"There must be more people here then. It can't just be him. Maybe he brought his family?"

"I don't know...I guess we can ask Miss An'Tufal."

"He doesn't have family," Clea said, startling Meagan. "At least, as far as the public knows. He was solely devoted to his work."

"You have a light footstep," Meagan muttered. "But take a look at this place. Do you really think he lives here all alone?"

"It's very possible. Sometimes, genius flourishes best away from all distractions."

Rudy got on the com. "Hang tight, we're landing now."

The ship turned and as it did, Meagan noted a man standing near the doors of the structure. The landing pad was attached to the main area through a bridge easily large enough for a couple of cargo containers to travel side by side. As they set down, the engines whined while setting to idle.

Meagan performed a systems check and filed a positive report. She nodded to Rudy who turned to Clea. "We're good to go, Miss An'Tufal. Ship's secure."

"Thank you." Clea turned away. "I think at least one of us should stay with the ship but if one of you is particularly curious, please feel free to come with."

"You want to go?" Rudy offered. "I'm not curious."

"Yeah, I think I will." Meagan took off her safety harness and followed Clea out. "Don't get bored without us!"

Clea entered the mess area and Meagan followed. "We're here. I'll remind you again, let me do the talking. Once we establish the possibility of Durant having our storage device, I'll negotiate him letting us have it. The rest of you are just there to observe. Do you have any questions before we leave?"

"Are we going armed?" Jenks asked.

"Side arms only, please."

"You sure?" Walsh lifted his brows. "It didn't work out for us so well last time and now we've got some better hardware."

"Durant should be the only person here. Even if he's not, these won't be pirates so we shouldn't experience any sort of…rioting. Let's go. I think he's waiting for us."

***

Clea steadied herself as they dropped the ramp and headed out into the cool air. The scent of pine tickled her nose, something she didn't expect. She hadn't experienced those types of trees except on Earth. To find them out here, and in such a large number, seemed strange. She turned and started down the lane leading to the massive complex.

The distance was only a few hundred meters but it looked much farther. The sound of the waterfall cascading nearby and the wind blowing through the trees felt soothing and she understood why Durant might've taken up there. He definitely found a tranquil place to do whatever task he put himself to.

Sunlight beamed down, filtered through sparse clouds. It made the area bright as it glistened off the shiny metal walls of the structure and the light gray of the paved walkway. Despite the light, the ambient temperature sat around sixty-five degrees. Clea wondered what season the region might be in. Without blossoming plants or more deciduous trees, it was hard to tell without a scan.

The others followed close behind with the marines taking up the rear. Crandy, Jessy, Arak and Meagan were enthralled enough to be admiring the scenery like true tourists. Clea kept her focus on the man waiting for them.

He dressed in a long, gray coat with matching pants and a black shirt. His hair was jet black with streaks of white on the sides. He wore a beard, also flecked with gray and he stood motionless as they approached. Clea's eyes flicked to the side and noted turrets over the nearby doorway. A green light indicated they were active.

"Durant Vi'Puren," Clea called as they drew close enough to be heard. "Thank you for seeing us, I appreciate it more than you know."

"You'll have to convince me this wasn't a mistake to let you come here," Durant replied. "What do you want? And however did you become…well…this?"

"I can explain everything," Clea said, "but our primary need is a storage device you may have procured. Some pirate group or scavengers stripped a storage device from the *Tempered Steel*. The ship was destroyed in a battle with an enemy you possibly know better than any other civilian alive."

"Ah." Durant shook his head. "And who told you I might have it?"

Clea gestured to Crandy, who stepped forward looking sheepish. "Uh...hi, sir." Crandy waved. "Sorry I told them about you but I didn't have a lot of choice. The alliance showed up and destroyed our base. They were taking prisoners! I had to get out of there and this was the price."

"You're a fool, Crandy," Durant replied. "These people aren't pirates."

Crandy scowled. "What does that mean?"

"They're clearly military." Durant gestured to Clea. "And I know her parents. She'd never turn criminal."

"Is this true?" Crandy turned to Clea. "Are you...are you alliance?"

"Yes," Clea said. "But we'll honor our bargain with you. You're not going to prison."

"But there's no planet of wealth then..." Crandy clenched his fists. "I'm ruined!"

"Just imagine where you'd be if we hadn't taken you," Jenks said.

"And where would *you* be without me?" Crandy shouted. "Certainly not standing here you insignificant military lapdog!"

"Settle down," Jessy said. "This is a chance to start over, for both of us. Don't throw it away."

"You shut up!" Crandy pointed at the pirate. "You brought them to me in the first place! This is your fault!"

Durant held up his hands. "That's enough. Crandy, if these people genuinely have good cause to be here, I'll reward you myself. But they'd better have a good story."

"We do," Clea assured him.

"Then come with me." Durant turned back toward the complex. "Let's get indoors where we can speak with some decorum."

***

Gray anxiously checked the reports, waiting for an opportunity to bow out of the operation and get moving. He wanted to chase after Clea as soon as possible, to give them the backup they might sorely need. Unfortunately, the semantics of collecting so many prisoners and all that evidence simply took time.

Olly worked past his shift in order to help locate every scrap of information on the surface of the planet. He uncovered three hidden caches of contraband, directing the alliance forces so they could confiscate them. He even managed to download the schematics for the weapon the pirates used against them.

Hopefully we can build a defense against those. Maybe it would work on the enemy. Lots of possibilities there.

Olly yawned and stretched, pausing in his motion. Gray looked at him, recognizing the hesitation to move. The man saw something and that meant they should all brace themselves for some bad news.

"Captain, some ship just jumped out of here...one we didn't detect until a moment ago."

"What do you mean? How'd we miss it?"

"I'm checking the data..." Olly frowned. "Sir, I think they were using something to deflect sensor probes. They must not be able to do it right before a jump—the energy build up may contradict the other tech...I'm totally guessing here but in any event, they literally appeared for a moment then jumped out of the system."

"Leonard, can you calculate a course?"

"Um..." Leonard took a moment, also having worked past the end of his shift. He paused. "They jumped out within five meters of where Miss An'Tufal's ship departed. We don't have a signature for them so I can't track where they went."

"You think they're chasing Clea?" Adam asked.

Gray shrugged. "It would be just our luck. Fortunately, we've been out here for hours so our team has a major head start. I hope they're ready to defend themselves if necessary."

"I'm sure they are. Meagan and Rudy are good combat pilots."

Gray nodded. "Still, we need to get moving as quickly as possible. Agatha, contact the alliance command ship. Tell them we're on a schedule and we need to get moving. Redding, begin the countdown for a jump. I want us at those coordinates in the next twenty minutes. Let's get our people back."

Chapter 11

The wonders in Durant's workshop shocked Clea. They wondered how he might've built such a place all alone but he wasn't entirely. Robots with fully articulated joints and movement for work, occupied his factory. They brought his visions to life on an assembly line, crafting the communication tower and living quarters as well as all the labs for further research.

Some of them were designed for mining, delving deep into the earth all around the area. The trees came as saplings a short time ago but through chemical assistance and terraforming, Durant got them to grow into a vast forest. It provided a natural deterrent for the heavy winds during the winter months and an endless supply of wood for the foundry.

The minerals they pulled and used were of the highest quality, many of which were used in alliance space vessels. He experimented on weapons and quality of life devices to take away the needs of every day labor. Artificial intelligence drove the machines all night long while he rested and in the morning, he checked the logs to correct any errors.

Over the years, he perfected the systems, creating a working rhythm that allowed him to conduct his research *and* apply it practically. He showed them some of the weapons labs as they walked, rooms full of guns enough for an army. Many of them required no ordinance and fired beams from packs which recharged within seconds. They were good for a thousand shots but he was aiming for more.

When asked why he would put so much thought into the weapons when he left because of the war, he had a simple enough answer.

"My critics wanted to blame the war on me," Durant explained. "They protested my involvement and were of the impression that if I stopped designing weapons, the fighting would simply stop. That naivety wore on me. Most of them were young and didn't remember my work prior to the conflict. If they had, they'd know my focus had always been on *saving* lives, not taking them.

"I needed a place to work in peace. I want to stop the war, Clea but I couldn't do so with protestors hounding me every step of the way. So I bide my time...however, I'm not ready to share this with the alliance just yet. There's still too much to do. I don't understand the enemy yet. That's why I study every battle. I've made breakthroughs...but not solved the problem."

"Have you studied the battle I'm here about?" Clea asked.

"I have so many black boxes and storage devices, I've barely scratched the surface," Durant said. "Crandy might've told you I haven't bought anything in months. My computers are processing it all, some of the best technology ever built and even they cannot scour the data fast enough to go through it all quickly. In short, I doubt I've seen what you're looking for yet but if I have, it didn't contain the epiphany you're hoping for."

"I suppose we'll see." Clea sighed.

They reached the primary complex, Durant's living space. The foyer was well appointed and comfortable, with plush furniture and a massive fireplace filled with blazing flames. Clea admired the rustic decor offsetting the hyper technology all around them. It felt homey despite the foundry not even three hundred meters away.

Sound proofing took away all the noise of labor, leaving this place tranquil. Durant led them through the room and down a hallway to a computer lab. Databanks lined the walls and a single terminal with twelve screens occupied the center opposite the door. He moved over and sat down, entering a thirty digit password.

The screens came to life, displaying information on an OS Clea had never seen before. *He does everything. No wonder everyone spoke so highly of him. His knowledge is impressive to say the least.*

"These storage devices you see around the room are my sorters. They're linked up to a warehouse on the other side of this wall holding literally countless banks of information. It took three months to index my initial findings and it's an ongoing continual process. After nearly a year, just about everything is searchable but as far as finding specific bits...that will take a lot more time."

"Maybe we won't need it," Clea said. "Can you relate anything you've learned about the enemy so far? Do you understand how they operate?"

"I know what their ships are made of, how they power them and the structural integrity of their shields," Durant explained. "I wrote a paper on their tactics, both before I left and after. The latter piece will be something you can leave with. Even if I'm not ready, it'll help your commanders fight the battle."

Crandy groaned. "I can't believe you guys are military…"

"Just stop," Jenks grunted. "Be happy you're alive."

"Anyway," Durant continued, "tell me what you're after and we can try to find it."

"We're looking for a battle involving a ship called the *Tempered Steel*. You might have the storage device I used to keep my data."

Durant turned to her, raising a brow. "And what exactly do you believe you're going to find?"

"I served on the ship on my first tour as a tech officer," Clea said. "We got into a battle, eight of us against four of them. We lost three ships as did they. I was injured when we took a direct hit and had to evacuate. Frankly, I lost my memory of the entire event until a few days ago when I had a dream."

"A dream." Durant shook his head. "A dream brought you all this way?"

"In a manner of speaking, yes. My psychologist warned me my memories may never return or, if they did, it could be through a dream or some other trauma. Fortunately for me, it didn't involve anything uncomfortable. Anyway, during the mission, I found something during the attack. A signal and I believe it may help us."

"If that's true, I'll certainly devote some cycles to studying the recuperative power of sleep." Durant began typing, watching one of the screens. "This may take a moment so you'll forgive me if—"

An alarm went off overhead, causing Crandy and Jessy to jump.

"Um…what is that?" Jenks asked.

Durant tapped something on his console. One of the terminals depicted a shot of space, a satellite image showing a large ship approaching orbit. "We have uninvited guests."

"Who are they?" Meagan leaned in. "That's not the enemy."

"No," Durant said. "They're mercenaries I believe. Someone who followed you here perhaps."

"How?" Clea asked. "We jumped. How would they have sophisticated enough equipment to plot our jump course?"

Durant shook his head. "Silly girl. Pirates have all sorts of black market software. It's not hard to snatch the coordinates from a computer just before the jump. It's how they catch merchants who think they can escape."

A smaller vessel detached from the larger. "That's a troop transport," Walsh pointed out. "Don't you have defenses?"

Durant nodded. "Some of the best but I'm afraid they're not working. I'm actually very impressed. These scum managed to disable the orbital turrets in record time. Their tech officer is amazing...perhaps I was wrong. They may not be mercenaries. Let's see...there's a symbol on the side of that ship. A couple of circles intersecting. I've never seen it before, have you?"

Crandy's shoulders slumped. "I have. They call themselves *Orion's Light*.Those zealot bastards visited our bases before, demanding weapons and improvements at half the cost they're worth...sometimes even bigger discounts. I've seen them simply take things from vendors."

"Who are they?" Jenks asked. "What's their deal?"

"They're some kind of psychotic order," Crandy replied. "A bunch of crazies that are against everyone. Probably taking a page from the enemy you guys are so keen to fight to be honest. They don't believe in the alliance or any other culture. Their sole purpose is to eventually run the galaxy as a religious state."

"And yet they consort with pirates," Meagan said. "Seems hypocritical."

"They're also about getting the job done through any means necessary," Crandy replied.

"I've run into them too," Jessy said. "They're real scum and they'll kill anyone. Women, children...whatever they have to do to get their point across."

"How have you *alliance* types never heard of them?" Crandy glared at Clea. "I mean, your intel must be terrible."

"There are far too many fringe groups for us to track them all," Clea replied. "They can crop up any time and anywhere as long as someone has the resources to fund them. And clearly, they've managed to procure some better than average tech people if they got past Durant's defenses."

"Anyway, why are they here?" Walsh asked. "Wait...don't bother. They want the gear."

"Yes, it would be quite the boon to their cause," Durant said. "Clea, the system is quite simple to search. I'll leave you here to find the data you're after."

"What're you going to do?" Clea asked.

"Help your friends defend this place," Durant turned to the others. "I hope you're interested in making this happen."

Arak nodded. "We can do whatever is necessary. Let us break into the weapon stores and we'll set up the defenses."

"Very good. You might want to radio back to your ship. Whoever you left behind is probably going to contact you at any moment. Let's hope we can manage their numbers. This fight is likely to be quite bloody."

***

Jenks leaned close to Walsh as they followed Durant. "I recognize that symbol they showed us."

Walsh whispered back, "from where?"

"Think back to the fight with those jerks who burst out on us as we left Crandy's shop. They had patches on their sleeves."

"Your attention to detail is pretty sick because I didn't have a chance to admire their clothes while they shot at us."

"When I took their stuff, I noticed each of them wore one. They etched it on their guns too." Jenks scowled. "I'll show you when we get back to the ship. I don't think that was random and they weren't after us. They wanted Crandy."

"Because he had all those guns in the shop."

"Maybe," Jenks agreed. "Or maybe they knew about this place. Same destination as us, different reason."

"Seems plausible but what timing." Walsh shook his head. "Why didn't you tell Miss An'Tufal?"

"I run things by you first in case I'm crazy."

"Your mental state's a given but we'll have to brief her soon. Could be important." Walsh scratched his head. "I wonder. Crandy did say he'd seen those type of guys take stuff before. I wonder why he didn't say anything when they attacked us."

"Probably because, like you, he didn't notice the patches."

Walsh nodded. "Good point. Anyway, we should focus on not getting dead. I'd prefer to make it back from this mission alive, if it's all the same to you."

"Wouldn't have it any other way." Jenks grinned. "Besides, that's what we do, man. We've got this."

"I love your confidence," Walsh muttered. "Move out."

***

Rudy met the others near one of the large storehouses located by where they landed. Some of Durant's robots, absolute tech wonders, carried equipment out and stacked it nearby. Jenks and Walsh went about familiarizing themselves with the different weapons. Arak stood beside Durant, speaking with him quietly while Jessy and Crandy stayed out of the way.

"What's going on?" Rudy asked. "What're we doing?"

"Someone seems to have followed us," Meagan replied. "I'm scanning their vessel now."

"Shouldn't we get up there and take it out then?" Rudy gestured to their ship. "Our weapons are pretty nasty."

"Not a good plan," Durant interrupted. "In fact, I'm going to place a shield on your vessel so it doesn't take damage but if they were able to take down my defenses, then your craft won't be any match for their cannons. No, we'll make our stand on the ground."

"Can you arm the robots?" Arak asked.

"Kind of. Some of them will be outfitted with their own turrets but we'll be controlling them. However, I have a fear about it. My guess is that they found a way to do a precise EMP attack. That's how they knocked out the weapons above us. If that's the case, and they have something equally capable for ground engagements, they'll be able to take out the robots and we won't be able to adjust."

"Can't EMP this," Jenks said, holding up a large rifle. "I'm digging the idea that this thing doesn't need to be reloaded."

Durant nodded. "Yes, I suspect we should be listening to you two on where to setup."

"The fact is we don't want them shooting at the storehouse with all the armaments," Walsh said. "How do your shields work?"

"I've got plenty of them but they'll last roughtly five minutes each and can take quite a bit of kinetic punishment before failing. However, they are also subject to the concern about EMP."

"No problem," Jenks said. "These metal containers over here are full of resources, wood and metal. Let's get them moved out here and use them as cover. I'll get out there and throw some mines down. You don't think they're going to be so brazen as to land directly in the complex, do you?"

Walsh sighed. "They don't have much reason not to."

"I'll give them one," Durant replied, turning to his data pad. He hit a button and a section of the ceiling opened, revealing a massive cannon. He tapped at it a few times. "There, this is going to make their entry less than pleasant."

The gun began firing, massive red blasts which vanished into the sky. Rudy wondered if they might be capable of causing damage to the ship in orbit. They had such defenses on Earth now and they were incredibly powerful. He couldn't imagine a troop transport being capable of taking that kind of shot without going down.

Durant watched his scanner intently and Rudy held his breath, waiting for the man's report. Meanwhile, the robots helped build some cover and Jenks hurried out into the field beyond the foundation of the complex and planted the mines. Walsh armed Crandy and Jessy, giving them positions further down the line. Meagan took a rifle and found a doorway near the makeshift cover.

Rudy grabbed a gun and one of the larger shield generators. He hurried back to the ship and placed it underneath, engaging a delayed timer. It would turn on in thirty seconds and encompass the entire ship. The projector threw the beans around the vessel in a great dome, touching the ground. It should be safe, at least for the time behind.

That's our way home so I hope it stays that way.

When he got back, Durant smiled. "My attack's working. They are no longer on a direct course for my home."

"Where are they going to land?" Walsh shouted.

"About a thousand meters that way." Durant pointed. "In the forest. They'll have to trudge through the trees to get here."

"Any natural predators to worry about?" Meagan called.

"Not that will deter them," Durant replied. "They may be tired but that's all. However many men they bring, and I'll know the moment they open their ship, is how many we'll have to deal with."

Jenks came back, hurrying over to them. "I planted a bunch of mines and threw in some other nasty surprises. There are rocks on top of them, should act as a decent amount of shrapnel if they trigger any. Some are on remote detonators so we can let them rip from a data pad back here."

"Good idea," Walsh said. "Jenks and I will do the heavy lifting out here. You guys stick to the doorways and move about to different windows for better shots. Watch your line of fire and avoid this area. That's where we're going to cover. We'll need some grenades."

Jenks offered him a satchel. "There ya go."

Robots moved in front of them, each loaded up with a turret on its shoulders. They crouched down, their waists able to rotate, allowing a decent field of fire. Other turrets were setup along the edge of the landing, each one controlled by Durant's computer. He moved back into the warehouse and closed the door.

"Okay, the old dude's safe," Jenks turned to Rudy. "You should work with Miss Pointer." He gestured to Meagan. "Stay in that building over there. You'll have the best vantage to shoot guys coming from our flank to the east."

"On it." Rudy hurried over to the other pilot and entered the room. She had opened the window and poised her rifle on the edge, peering out into the forest. "They haven't landed yet but are you ready for this?"

"Not my personal choice for fighting," Meagan said, "but at least I remember how to aim."

"I really would rather be in the ship."

"Me too."

"Do you believe them about the weapons these guys have?"

Meagan shrugged. "It's not worth taking the chance. This Durant guy has some pretty incredible technology and our visitors blew right through his outer defenses. I'm thinking it's better to err on the side of caution this time."

Rudy nodded. He agreed but it didn't set well with him. The idea that they were about to be involved in a ground conflict turned his stomach. He'd been in plenty of scrapes, most of them with the Behemoth but this one was way outside his comfort zone. He hadn't fired a hand weapon at a person in a *long* time.

So long he couldn't remember.

This is going to work out. We're on course for a simple engagement. The people we have with us are good and that tech is going to provide us quite the advantage. Durant's a genius. We're going to be okay.

Crandy's voice crackled over their coms. "This is insane, you guys realize that, right? If there are dozens of them, we're going to be screwed!"

"How can there be dozens?" Jessy's voice answered.

"Because that's how they operate! I've seen it. They have far more people than brains. A bunch of brainwashed idiots with nothing to lose! That's what we're facing."

"Relax," Jenks said. "Just means they won't have any self preservation when we start shooting. Makes them a lot easier to kill."

"Says the marine who's probably killed more people than I've met," Crandy grumbled.

"Be quiet," Walsh's voice came up next. "They're about to land."

They saw the ship off in the distance, nearly a mile away. It came in fast, avoiding more shots from the cannon which stopped firing when they plunged into the trees. A moment passed before Durant spoke up into the microphone, his tone grave as he reported his findings. Rudy once again held his breath.

"I'm afraid they've brought thirty-six people in there," Durant announced. "Prepare yourselves. At a normal rate of speed, they should arrive in less than fifteen minutes."

Here we go. Rudy tried not to think about the enemy's numbers. He focused on the weapon in his hands, on what his task was and staying alive. In the next thirty minutes, he and his friends might well be dead...or worse. The only thing they could do now was hope and fight with everything they had. *Worst mission ever.*

Chapter 12

The Behemoth made their jump finally, leaving the system and following Clea's coordinates. As soon as they arrived, Gray was on his feet, standing beside Olly. The younger man performed a system scan while Leonard mapped the solar system for them. On a screen to the left, they saw the star and the different planets orbiting it.

"Contact," Olly said. "Large capital ship orbiting the second planet."

Gray frowned. "What's the origin?"

"Um…" Olly performed a database search. "Unknown. But they do have a symbol." He put it on the screen, two circles intersecting. "There you go."

"Any ideas?" Gray turned to Adam who shrugged.

"I've never seen it."

"Hail them," Gray said. "Let's see if they want to talk. And what's on that planet?"

Olly paused. "Our people must be down there. I have their shuttle on scans."

"Get them on the line too."

"No response from the unknown vessel," Agatha said. "I've got Clea on channel seven."

Gray went to his station and brought Clea up on his speaker. "Report. What's going on down there?"

"Sir, we may have found the data," Clea answered. "I'm glad to hear from you. We're about to be attacked by a group of zealots calling themselves *Orion's Light*. They followed us here from the pirate planet, intent on taking...well, whatever they want."

"I see. They don't seem to be firing."

"They've landed a force on the planet to take the facility intact." Clea paused. "I'm searching for the data while the others prepare to defend the location. We've got turrets and decent hand ordinance but numbers are lacking. We're looking at over thirty combatants."

"We'll get you some help, Clea, standby." Gray turned to Adam. "Work with Marshall and Revente to get some people down there ASAP. Agatha, give them one more try on hail. Tell them if they do not back off, we *will* open fire."

Agatha relayed the message and Adam went about his task. Gray turned to Redding and gestured. "Get us in range for an attack. I want to be ready to hit them the moment we have to. Olly, can you tell us how they're armed?"

"Like the pirates." Olly sighed. "Potentially worse. Their shields are on par with our own. They can take some hits...and they might be able to dish out some serious damage. Plus, their hull...it's made of something particularly powerful. I think it's designed for ramming."

"Again with the ramming!" Gray clenched his fist. "Okay, work with Redding to plot the best places to hit them. I want maximum damage potential when this goes hot. Sound the alert through the ship and get all pilots on ready. Those people down there don't have a lot of time and if we don't get them some reinforcements, they're going to have a real bad day."

***

Revente gave the briefing in person, a rarity as most of the time they received their mission parameters while in the cockpits of their fighters, waiting to launch. Mick carried his helmet under his arm, standing amidst his fellows on the hangar deck. Each of them exchanged glances, unsure about the change in protocol.

As the Group Commander took his place in front of them, he addressed them quickly. "Team, we're sending you out in support of efforts against a different kind of enemy. Not the one who invaded Earth or the new culture we encountered. These people are zealots, a fringe group bent on toppling governments.

"I'm bringing you together this way to express the gravity of the situation. While this ship may not seem all that imposing, they have weapons we're not entirely familiar with yet. We already know they have the same beam cannon the pirates used to take the Behemoth's shields down quickly. What other tricks they're hiding up their sleeves, we don't know.

"Use extreme caution as you fly today. You're not up there for attack but rather support. If they throw something at the Behemoth you can shoot down, do it. If they have fighters, you'll engage but until you're directed, *do not* assault the vessel directly. Wait for the shields to go down and the command. Bombers squadrons are to steer clear of the Behemoth and wait for orders.

"Do you have any questions?"

One of the pilots raised his hand, "sir, do we have any idea of what the enemy defenses are like?"

"They have shields on par with our own," Revente said. "Their hulls are also well armored and the bow is shaped for ramming. Next question?"

"Do we have clearance for Targets of Opportunity?"

"Negative. Wait for orders or call in what you see. I'll make the decision on the fly."

"Why not try the bombs right away?"

"We don't want to waste ordinance," Revente replied. "Throwing those away would be pointless if the shields just stop them."

No one else spoke up and Revente nodded. "Get to your ships and good luck."

Mick led his people to their fighters and boarded his own. They were the first with clearance and launched right away. As they left the ship, they pulled far enough away to avoid any secondary explosions from splash weapons. Directing themselves to face the enemy, he took in the threat.

They looked like most capital ships, long with weapon ports and a section near the middle for the bridge section. He noted they still hadn't broken orbit, still hadn't acknowledged the threat the Behemoth posed. Engagement might change their attitude. Something about their disregard annoyed Mick.

I hope you guys don't have anything to back up this arrogance.

Revente pinged them all, his voice filling their helmets. "The hull's opening," he said. "Looks like there're fighters after all."

Wow, for a fringe group, these guys are well funded! Hosting fighters isn't cheap!

Mick checked his scanner and counted twenty total flying to meet them. The Behemoth crew still outnumbered them but perhaps that didn't matter. The *Orion's Light* only needed to hold them off long enough to get what they wanted from the planet then they could flee. They must've believed whatever they'd find on the surface could be worth losing some of their own.

"As they clear their vessel, you're clear to engage," Revente called out. "Keep it tight and remember, we don't know what they've got. Your shields might not help. Keep it cautious."

Like hell.

Mick radioed to his own wing. "You heard him. Let's pair up and tear them down. Watch how they approach. It may tell a lot about them."

They separated out into groups of three. Six pulled off from the whole, heading toward the Behemoth. Mick scowled and called it in. One of their wing broke off to face those stragglers as the rest of them continued their approach on the mainstay of the enemy fighters. Distance closed rapidly, numbers plunging on the scanner.

The enemy opened fire, purple blasts tearing past Mick's ship. He veered to the left, his wingman following closely. He jammed the throttle forward, initiated the top thrusters and plunged forward, redirecting to gain a firing solution. The enemy was fast but he just managed a good couple shots at the one lagging behind.

A series of pulse blasts caught the tail, igniting the engine. The ship began to spin just as an explosion popped the fuselage. It went up in an instant, annihilating the cockpit before the pilot could pull the ejection handle. His two companions turned, engaging with Mick and Shelly.

Hitting his thrusters, Mick tried to pull away but it became apparent his pursuers matched him in speed. Shelly directed him to pull up, to draw them away. He yanked on the stick, his thrusters pulling his nose up. One of the two fighters climbed after him, the other tried to stay on Shelly.

Mick saw his scanner out of the corner of his eye. Shelly hit the reverse thrusters and dropped behind her attacker. Blasts made Mick wince as she took out her target. The one behind him fired, nearly tagging him if not for a quick evasion. He dodged with a jolted thrust pushing him down just enough to avoid destruction.

Disengaging his engine's safety link, he initiated the left thrusters, spinning his vessel while still maintaining his momentum. Depressing the trigger, he fired in his opponent's path, scoring a direct hit to the side. Shields flared but the ship reacted, a knee jerk reaction pulling him away from his pursuit.

Mick re-engaged the safety on his engines and struggled against the inertia, even as the dampeners whined while compensating. He turned to his scanner, noting he was clear. Shelly closed in, reforming on him while he tried to get a visual of the target.

Explosions around him caused a major distraction, other fights broken out all across the sector. He noted at least three of their own had been taken out even as they were maintaining a solid upper hand. "I've got him!" Shelly called out. "Trying for our six again!"

"Break left and let's put him in a crossfire," Mick said. "Go!"

They burst away from one another, flying hard in a semi-circle. The enemy came between them and realized his mistake too late. He tried to plunge out of the way but Mick and Shelly fired at the same time, lighting him up from two directions. An orange ball erupted them went out, leaving nothing behind of the ship.

"Great work." Mick turned to get back into the fight, leading the way toward the others. "Looks like we've got some mop up still. Let's do this."

"Right behind you," Shelly paused. "Behemoth's about to engage. We need to steer clear of that nonsense."

"Panther Wing, regroup. Form up on us for another push."

The other ships closed in and he quietly thanked heaven they were all still with him. He didn't want to lose a pilot his first time out as commander and certainly didn't want to explain to Meagan what happened. As they plunged toward the remaining enemy, the scanner said only a half dozen remained.

Mick watched as one of Tiger Wing tore through one of the enemies, very nearly colliding with the debris. He winced as the ship barely pulled up in time, shields flaring as it contacted the jagged edges of metal. Another ship jet across his path and Mick had to pull up to avoid them.

More pulse blasts erupted around him. The dogfight turned totally chaotic. He let the targeting computer decide who to shoot at, pulling the trigger when he got tone. A hit, but not fatal. The enemy drifted away but did not eject. Another of his comrades finished him off. Only three opponents remained but instead of falling back or surrendering, they headed straight for the Behemoth, pushing to full throttle.

"What're they doing?" Someone's voice crackled in Mick's ear.

"They're going straight for it?" Shelly sounded shocked. "Why? What do they hope to accomplish?"

"Sensors read an overload in their reactors," Mick said. "They're turning themselves into bombs! Get after them and finish them off before they get there!"

Every fighter started in on pursuit, pushing to full throttle. A few random shots nearly hit but the enemy was moving too fast. They had only a few more chances before the ships-turned-missiles reached their target. Mick didn't know what kind of damage they'd cause but he didn't have any intention of finding out.

"Revente, you've got a problem we're trying to solve," Mick called out. "Three fighters incoming hot. They're suiciding."

"Roger that," Revente replied. "Take them down but we'll get the defenses ready for it."

I hope that's true, Mick thought. *We've tried this tactic before to great effect.*

***

Redding moved them into position and finally, the enemy broke orbit, directing themselves into the Behemoth's path. A blue field erupted around them, indicating their opponent had raised shields. Olly called it out, letting them all know a real fight was about to begin. The fighters had already engaged.

The *Orion's Light* ship made up their mind. No communication, just a straight fight. They didn't even know what they were up against and still planned to throw down. The notion made Redding shake her head. Why not at least *try* to talk? Why not see what someone had to say? Buy some time for their attack crews on the planet but no, they went straight to escalate.

"Scans are in," Olly said. "They've got pulse cannons equivalent of our own and...yes, those beam weapons we encountered with the pirates."

"*Weapons*?" Adam asked. "Do you mean they have more than one?"

"Yes, sir, they're sporting two." Olly shook his head. "Nasty combo."

Gray hummed. "Do you have a range on them?"

"According to our last encounter, they needed to be at close range," Olly said. "If we remain at least twenty-thousand kilometers distant, they'll be forced to only use their pulse weapons. But...I have some bad news."

"Can't wait," Redding muttered.

"Their engines are powerful. I'd say they've sacrificed a lot of luxury for extra generators and power. They're smaller than us but they've got equal defenses, slightly superior firepower and more maneuverability."

"And if they're truly zealots," Gray said, "then there's a good chance they lack much in the way of self preservation. Did you get us any good targeting?"

Olly shrugged. "I mean, the whole ship's made up of energy relays and weapons. I can't find any particular weaknesses. We're going to have to beat them down, sir."

"You heard him, Redding. When they get in range, light them up."

"They're hailing us, sir," Agatha said. "They've demanded our immediate surrender."

Redding turned a wide eyed expression to Gray. "They're serious, aren't they?"

"I'll let you give our answer, Redding." Gray leaned back in his seat. "Fire at will."

"Yes, sir."

Redding turned to her station, marking a series of proposed targets. Olly guessed on them but they were better than nothing. One aimed for the bridge, another what he believed to be a weapon relay and another, the presumed life support system. *Wow, you're pretty vicious, Oliver. Let's hope this works.*

The computer lit up, lights blinking to indicate they were within range. Redding fired, launching the cannons in stages. As she counted them off, the second barrage following the first at a good ten seconds. The third, ten seconds after that. This allowed her to have a downtime of only fifteen seconds for the recharge before she could shoot again.

All the work the engineers did back on Earth provided the extra power to make this possible, to enhance the weapons and optimize the energy output. The first of the blasts connected with the enemy, splashing on their shields. She reversed their thrusts as the second pulse beams struck home.

"Direct hits," Olly spoke calmly but Redding heard the tension in his voice. "Shields holding. I'm reading eighty percent."

"Not bad," Gray said. "Keep our distance, Redding."

The enemy returned fire, shots slamming into the Behemoth, causing the mildest of trembles. "We're holding…ninety-five percent. Enemy is gaining."

Leonard cleared his throat. "Captain, I've laid in a course for a microjump. According to Lieutenant Darnell's calculations, their special weapon has a forty-five degree angle arc so if we end up behind them, they'll have to turn to get a shot off."

"Understood," Gray said. "When they're within range, perform the jump and lay into them. Maybe direct shots to the thrusters wont' be as protected."

The ship shook again, this time more violently. "Another set of hits," Olly said. "Shields are down to eighty percent, recharging fast."

Redding fired again but held back the second and third barrages. The enemy was closing fast, at nearly full thrust. She watched the sensors closely, waiting for the last moment to engage the jump.

"Those special weapons are powering up," Olly said. "They'll have a firing solution in less than five seconds."

"Jump," Gray said. "Now!"

Redding slapped the button, gripping the edge of her console. The ship trembled, shimmered and a moment later, the view screen changed, depicting the enemy's rear. "Try that, you bastards." She fired, this time every cannon at the same time directly into the enemy engines.

"Enemy shields down to forty percent!" Olly shouted. "They're attempting to turn!"

"Divert power to recharge," Gray said. "Get us some energy before they can take their shot."

"Working on it, sir." Redding worked the controls, contacting engineering for the auxiliary power they needed. As the meter began to rise, she kicked the thrusters on to pull back again, this time toward the planet. They needed twenty seconds for another firing solution but their enemy was fast and they were already showing their side to them.

The jump module was also on cool down. Another minute for another such trick. Redding willed the weapons to come back online and then, her primary cannons lit up green. She fired, a full blast with tremendous results. Shields flickered and a micro explosion on the exterior of the enemy indicated an actual hit.

"Damage!" Olly shouted. "Minor, but we got through. Their shields are at thirty percent ship wide but...wait..."

"What is it?" Gray asked. "What's wrong?"

"Shields are recharging at an insane rate! They're up to fifty...sixty...I don't know what's happening."

"Fire again!" Gray ordered. "Do it now!"

Redding let loose another two volleys, collecting again with the now mostly recharged shields. Nothing got through but they did see the shields flare up, much like they might when they're being overloaded. "If we can keep that up, we might tear them down," Gray said. "Do they have a solution?"

"Almost!"

"Full thrust," Adam said. "Get us back from them!"

"We're at full thrust," Redding replied. "We're moving as fast as we can without taking away from the weapon recharge."

"They're about to fire!" Olly shouted.

Gray spoke over the ship wide intercom. "Brace for impact. I repeat, brace for impact."

Cannons on the front of the enemy brightened as red glows filled the barrels. They saw them turn, aiming directly for the Behemoth. Olly's hands moved frantically and Redding prepared for evasive. She checked the cool down on the jump module but it had another full thirty seconds.

Time moves too slowly and too fast in combat...this is probably going to hurt.

The enemy fired and the shields began flaring. Olly started calling out the damage and the countdown began on how long they could fire, whether the Behemoth would get out of the beams path or their shields dropped completely, exposing them to a pulse blast attack. Redding entered the cannons into the targeting computer, prepared to let loose their own fury in retaliation.

"Opening fire," Redding shouted out, pulling the trigger. As their attack shot forth from their cannons, she held her breath in anticipation of what she hoped might at least slow down the enemy assault. This moment may well determine the course of the rest of the battle. She took a brief moment to pray, then watched the sensors intently.

***

"Enemy contact," Durant's voice burst into Jenks's ear. "One click out. They're on sensors, moving fast. They'll be at your first mines in less than twenty seconds."

"Get ready," Jenks ordered, turning to Walsh. "Hold fire on the turrets for my mark. I'll detonate the mines just as they pass."

Cannons on the front of the enemy brightened as red glows filled the barrels. They saw them turn, aiming directly for the Behemoth. Olly's hands moved frantically and Redding prepared for evasive. She checked the cool down on the jump module but it had another full thirty seconds.

Time moves too slowly and too fast in combat...this is probably going to hurt.

The enemy fired and the shields began flaring. Olly started calling out the damage and the countdown began on how long they could fire, whether the Behemoth would get out of the beams path or their shields dropped completely, exposing them to a pulse blast attack. Redding entered the cannons into the targeting computer, prepared to let loose their own fury in retaliation.

"Opening fire," Redding shouted out, pulling the trigger. As their attack shot forth from their cannons, she held her breath in anticipation of what she hoped might at least slow down the enemy assault. This moment may well determine the course of the rest of the battle. She took a brief moment to pray, then watched the sensors intently.

***

"Enemy contact," Durant's voice burst into Jenks's ear. "One click out. They're on sensors, moving fast. They'll be at your first mines in less than twenty seconds."

"Get ready," Jenks ordered, turning to Walsh. "Hold fire on the turrets for my mark. I'll detonate the mines just as they pass."

"Sounds good." His partner stood beside him, holding two grenades. They were ready to arm, prepped to throw when the enemy drew close enough for them. Several tense minutes passed between when the *Orion's Light* soldiers landed and when they finally drew close enough to engage. Adrenaline took over as the action was about to begin.

Jenks laid out mines a good twenty feet apart out in the woods, spreading them so when they detonated they'd cause the most amount of collateral damage. Considering who made them, he wouldn't be surprised if they took down some trees with the force of the blast. A little extra chaos would help the cause for sure.

Durant counted down in his ear from five. The soldiers moved far more cautiously than they anticipated, tactically rather than rushing in. *Where'd these guys train? They can't be ex-military, can they? Maybe their command structure is. Regardless, they certainly seem to know what they're doing. Getting past that cannon should've been impossible.*

"Two…" Durant said. "One. They have passed the mines."

Jenks hit the detonator, causing a series of massive explosions just beyond the trees. Men screamed, and a tree did, indeed go down. Walsh followed up, hurling his grenades out as far as he could. The two marines aimed their rifles over their cover, waiting to see if any of the soldiers made it out.

"You got five of them," Durant said. "They must've caught wind of the trap moments before it went off to spread out so quickly."

Great, they've got a sixth sense. "Understood," Jenks grumbled. The news disappointed him. He'd hoped to get a much larger contingent of them. As the grenades went off, he heard indistinct shouts, syllables without meaning. He glanced at Walsh who shrugged. "What the hell are they saying? Is that another language?"

"Battle language," Jessy said. "I've heard people talk about it before but never heard anyone actually use it. That must be what you're hearing."

Wow, these freaks developed their own language on top of it all. Fantastic.

"Contact," Walsh spoke softly. Jenks *felt* the tension in the rest of the team as they let it sink in what they just heard. "Two to our left flank."

Jenks scanned the area and paused, nodding once. He saw the men emerging, keeping their center of gravity low. They led with their weapons, pressed against their shoulders while staring down the sites. He shifted his own aim, marking them both. "Hold your fire, everyone. The explosions put them on edge but we need them to get closer if we hope to seal this deal."

"I've got some," Rudy said. "Um...contact right. Three incoming near the landing pad."

"We're on those," Meagan said. "They seem to be checking out the ship."

"Hold..." Jenks again kept his voice calm and low. He had some faith in Rudy and Meagan because he knew they were trained. The other three, Arak, Jessy and Crandy, on the other hand, might as well have been total civilians in his eyes. "Durant, do you have the targets?"

"Only dead ahead," Durant replied. "Six dead ahead of our defenses."

"Let me know when they're open and we'll let go."

Jenks took a deep breath, perhaps the last one he would be afforded for some time. He scowled at the men who continued to inch their way closer, wary of an ambush but forced to make progress. They didn't have the ability to take this place slowly. Not with the Behemoth topside causing their ride trouble.

"I have a shot," Durant said.

"All units!" Jenks shouted, hoping to startle their opponents. "Open fire!"

They didn't have time to try out the weapons Durant provided and Jenks didn't know exactly what to expect. It annoyed him, going into battle without at least pealing off a few rounds but he had to trust the guy and hope they worked as well as he said. When he depressed the trigger, the gun exhibited so little recoil, he wondered if he left a safety on.

Bright flashes erupted from the barrel and his first three rounds clipped a tree, chewing bark off as easily as a chainsaw might. The next burst caught one of his targets full in the chest, tossing him back on the ground with a smoldering hole where his heart used to be. The dead soldier's partner tried to dive for cover but Jenks caught him in the leg just above the knee.

The man got to cover but left his shin and foot behind. *Holy crap! This gun is insane!*

Jenks grabbed a grenade, cooked it for three seconds and threw it where the man tried to hide. Even with such a grievous injury, he represented a clear threat. Two arms and consciousness could still take some shots at them. The man cried out, this time not using their special language. The world help half way left his mouth before the grenade silenced him.

Seven down so far. Only twenty-nine to go. This is going to take a while.

The turrets went off, barking as they chewed through any natural cover out there, ripping people to shreds. Jenks aimed but did not fire, letting the defenses do their work. The victims were torn in half, ripped up by the high caliber rounds. Durant had the robots move, spreading out to flank anyone out there.

"Grenade!" Walsh shouted, ducking behind the cover. Jenks joined him but instead of an explosion, they heard a loud crack like someone struck wood with metal.

"Targeted EMP," Durant said. "The robots are down."

That was fast!

"Mister Vi'Puren," Arak's voice came over the com, "I have an idea for an EMP shield which could prevent such an attack in the future."

"It would need to be at the core level as my technology is already covered for such an attack."

"Not the time for a debate!" Jenks popped back up and started firing, catching a man in the head.

"We got ours on the right!" Rudy shouted. "But more are incoming! They're using the ship's shield for cover!"

"Just keep up the pressure," Jenks said between shots. "They can take cover all they want. It just wastes their time, not ours."

Walsh threw another pair of grenades then followed up with a few well timed bursts. Jenks knew who was shooting by the length of their shots. When he heard more than five rounds go off at once, it had to be Jessy or Crandy. The pilots had better sense. He and Walsh never went above three.

When the enemy finally returned fire, they had to drop down to cover. A concentrated current of suppressive shots made them keep their heads down. *If they keep this up, they'll definitely overrun us.* Jenks checked his own scanner and saw the men were definitely advancing. They need to find a way to stop them quick.

"Durant, you got any other tricks up your sleeve? And those of you behind cover at the doors, I need you to reposition and start clipping these guys!"

"I'm about to unleash another bout of turrets. These won't be as easy to take out for them...certainly not with their EMP."

"Don't wait on our account," Walsh shouted. "Get them going! Now!"

Turrets fired up, making a loud whine as they drove the attackers back into their cover once again. Walsh peeked out the side and took some shots, calling out hits. "Looks like we got another four or five of them."

Crandy cried out. "I'm hit! I'm hit!"

"I've got him," Jessy said. "Oh my God...this is bad!"

"Do what you can," Jenks replied. "We can't break off for him now. Stabilize and hope we get out of this in one piece to save him."

"I have bad news," Durant said. "We've got another troop transport bearing the sign of *Orion's Light*."

"Reinforcements?" Walsh sighed. "Christ, I can't believe they thought they needed them."

"We should be flattered," Jenks said. "Concentrate your fire and we'll get out of this, everyone! Keep them back!" Even as he gave the speech, he didn't entirely believe it. The thought they could stand against a second wave of these guys sounded ludicrous. He prepared himself for the last fight he may ever be in and continued firing.

Chapter 13

"Shields are at thirty percent!" Olly shouted. Sparks burst from panels overhead but none of them had time to take note. "They're still going strong!"

Gray gritted his teeth, thinking through the next few moments. The attack might well take out their defenses, leaving them open to catastrophic damage. But in mere seconds, their own attack would impact the enemy weapons, possibly giving them a reprieve. If so, they needed to take advantage of the fact and make it count.

"Time to jump module recharge?"

"On hold," Olly said. "Weapons took priority and our shields tapped the generators."

"Take that *off* hold," Gray ordered. "We need to hop if we're going to survive this."

"I have bad news," Adam said. "Revente just said the last three enemy fighters overloaded their reactors and charged us. His people are in pursuit now."

"Can we target them?"

"Possibly, but they're moving pretty fast. It's likely the pilots already killed themselves they're pushing so many G forces." Adam shook his head. "They're on autopilot."

Gray tilted his head. "Olly, are they locked on to us?"

"Yes, sir. I've picked up the signal." Olly paused. "Solid hit from our attack...the weapon stopped!" Shields holding at fifteen percent and recharging! Jump module will be back in ten seconds."

Gray nodded. "Redding, get us moving, close on the enemy."

Redding engaged the thrusters. "You want to get closer to them, sir?"

"Yeah, as if we're going to give them a broadside."

"This sounds risky," Adam said. "I think I know what you're planning."

"A microjump might save our lives. If it comes up in time." Gray turned to Olly. "How long before those ships to hit us?"

"Twenty seconds."

"Talk about cutting it close," Leonard muttered. "Course, sir?"

"Put us three-hundred thousand kilometers out away from the planet," Gray said. "Make it fast. Have Revente's people back off."

Leonard's hands rushed over the panel. "Course laid in and ready, sir."

"Initiate on my mark."

"Pilots have fallen back, Captain," Adam said. "They're moving to a safe range."

Olly spoke up, "enemy is firing again. This time, pulse cannons. Their other weapon must be on cool down, sir. Direct hit!"

The ship shook violently and something else sparked behind them, more overloaded circuits. "That took us down to *five percent* shields!" Olly pounded his terminal. "I'm trying to recharge faster but we can't at the expense of the jump module."

"What're their shields at?" Adam asked.

"Sixty percent." Olly sighed. "How are they doing that? How can they get them recharged so quickly?"

"We'll find out from the salvage." Gray turned to Redding. "Get ready."

Gray watched the countdown on the screen. "Fire our weapons just before we jump. It'll give them something else to think about for a moment."

"Sir, they're attempting to move off," Leonard called out.

"Fire and jump."

Redding slapped the trigger then hit the jump module. The ship shimmered, rattled and the screen changed, depicting a distant shot of the enemy. Three explosions racked the side, brightening space until Gray had to look away for a moment. "Get us back in there," Gray ordered. "Open fire as soon as we're in range."

"Enemy shields are totally down!" Olly said. "They're on auxiliary power it looks like. Wow…those reactors really went up."

"Agatha, give them a chance to surrender." Gray turned in his seat. "Hurry."

"You are ordered to surrender now and prepare to be boarded," Agatha said. "Power down your weapons and heave to. Repeat, you are ordered to surrender…ah!" She cried out just as the enemy vessel exploded on their screen, turning into a molten ball then winking out of existence.

"What the hell just happened?" Adam asked. "Olly?"

"Sir, they seem to have initiated a self destruct sequence." Olly read several things on his screen and nodded. "Yes, that was all them. The damage was bad but recoverable. Just before the explosion, I read that their weapons were offline and unavailable."

"I guess they didn't want to give up," Adam said. "Zealots, right?"

Gray nodded. "Search and rescue teams out in five. Let's see if any of them are left. Get our troop transports down to the surface to support our folks. Get Clea on the line again and bring our pilots back in. Time to mop this operation up and call it a day."

***

Clea worked as fast as she could, trying desperately to ignore the gunfire barking outside. She turned down the conversation of her team mates as they fought off the invaders. Their chatter distracted her from looking through the countless archives Durant compiled. As she tapped away, she began to worry she wouldn't find what she was after.

"Clea, this is Agatha on the Behemoth. Can you read me?"

"I do," Clea said. "But I'm a little busy right now. What's going on?"

"We've finished off the enemy ship and are sending down reinforcements to help you out. What's the situation?"

"Grave. They sent reinforcements as well."

"Can you hold?"

"They are so far," Clea replied. "I'm searching for the data now."

The door burst open behind her and she threw herself out of her chair just as a shot hit the wall opposite the monitors. She drew her side arm and shoved away with her feet, aiming in the direction of the attack. Two men entered slowly, one going right and the other left. She fired, connecting with a man's knee then shot twice more into his head.

The other fired wildly but missed, his shots going high and wide. She crawled toward the door for a better angle and leaned up to take a shot. Clean miss, near his back and he fired at the table she hid behind. Dropping to her back, bullets riddled the surface where she'd been moments before.

Rolling to her left, she aimed while lying on her back and shot again. The man screamed and rushed the door. She fired after him but missed. He seemed to be nursing his arm as he ran but she couldn't be sure. Clea climbed to her feet and sealed the room, locking it down before checking the man she'd shot before.

He was truly dead so she hurried back to the terminal and continued her search, trying to calm down. Her hands trembled as she typed.

"Are you okay?" Agatha's voice reminded her she'd been in a conversation a moment before. "What happened?"

"I was just attacked," Clea replied, "but I'm okay. How long before reinforcements arrive?"

"They're already en route and will land on your position."

"Have them coordinate with Jenks," Clea said. "That might not be the best plan. For whatever reason, we didn't use our ship in the fight so I think they're concerned about something."

"Roger, over and out."

Clea took a deep breath and continued working. She hoped the Behemoth soldiers got there in time. So much was riding on the success of this mission, even if the data wasn't present. Durant's research alone would set them years ahead in the arm's race. But if she found it...then they might be able to wrap the whole thing up.

If only it will be so easy. Come on, computer! Move! Move!

***

Jenks fired again and tapped Walsh. "We have to get back! Fall back to Meagan and Rudy!"

"That's going to be crazy, you know that, right?"

The enemy had begun laying down suppressive fire again, a wide spread of action all across the area. Bullets riddled their makeshift cover but so far, they hadn't employed any explosives. *I wonder why*. Jenks didn't want to look the gift horse in the mouth but considering the situation, it seemed suspicious.

They would be overrun if they didn't get to new cover but that meant risking being shot. His com barked in his ear. "This is Captain Hoffner, I understand you guys need some help."

Jenks felt his heart hammer in his chest. "Thank God! Glad to hear your voice, sir!"

"We've got two transport shuttles with fifty men converging on your location. What's your status?"

"Defenses are holding but not for long," Walsh replied. "We need to fall back to better cover. Enemy is about to overrun our position."

"Why didn't you use your ship for cover?"

"The enemy has some kind of directed EMP weapon," Jenks replied. "Could be possible to take a ship out of the air."

"Understood. Can we set down near your position safely?"

"I'll give you coordinates," Jenks said. "But we really need some help getting out of our current situation if you can risk it."

"We're on it. Stay alive, guys."

Jenks looked around and gestured to the door behind them. "It's only fifty meters away."

"Might as well be a mile," Walsh said. "They'll snag us, even with cover."

"They're *definitely* going to get us here and they aren't proving to be the best of shots."

A bullet nearly caught his foot and he pulled himself more fully behind the cover. Another scream echoed off behind *their* line, this time Jessy. "I've been hit!" He recovered himself quickly enough, not sounding as if he'd been butchered the way Crandy carried on. "Leg, I'll live."

"We've got a big problem!" Rudy shouted. "Grenade!"

There they are. Jenks cursed. They saved them for the buildings. "Get it out of there!"

He heard an explosion off to his left and prayed the pilots got it out of there. "Report!"

"We're okay," Meagan replied though a fit of coughing cut off her report. "Can't see a damn thing but we're okay!"

"For now!" Rudy cried out. "They're charging!"

"Shit!" Jenks turned and fired at the men he could see some seventy meters off. It caused them to divert their rush and run for the side of the building. He took two of them down before the other four made it to safety. A bullet grazed his arm and he winced, spinning to return fire. "We cannot stay out here!"

A ship flew by overhead and another opened up with a strafing run. More cries of agony filled the air and the strange battle language continued barking back and forth. Jenks and Walsh ran for it, each dashing at a full sprint. The door loomed ahead, growing larger with every step. When he cleared it, Jenks couldn't believe his luck. He swore they'd be gunned down in the effort.

Even more gunfire erupted outside, this time from the familiar rifles of their own men. Jenks glanced outside to help and saw as more than a dozen of their own took cover and laid down their own suppressive fire. The ship above flew by again but someone took a shot at it from a shoulder mounted weapon, a blue blast flying directly for it.

The pilot managed to evade the attack and disappeared behind Durant's home.

"That was an EMP blast," Durant pointed out. "If it would've hit them..."

"We get it." Jenks aimed and fired at the guy who tried to take down the ship. He connected with his shoulder and a second burst perforated his head. The man collapsed and as one of his friends tried to grab the weapon, Walsh blew him away. "Do you have another count on these guys?"

"There are ten left," Durant said. "My turrets are overheating."

Arak shouted for help but the cry was silenced a moment later. Jenks turned in time to see the man collapse to the ground, a wound in his head bleeding profusely. *Damn it!* He called out for a sound off. Meagan replied, "I'm okay, Rudy's down. Shot to the shoulder." Durant confirmed he was still okay.

Neither Crandy nor Jessy replied.

Wow, this is getting worse than I thought.

Jenks's arm hurt from where he'd been grazed. The wound stung and it ran up into his forearm but he did his best to ignore it. They were on the verge of driving these pricks back. All he had to do was hold out for a few more moments and they'd win. The miracle of their reinforcements arriving saved the day but they survived and that was no small feat.

More of the Behemoth's marines came from around the corner, charging into battle and firing into the ranks of the final men. Some of them tried to flee back toward their ship but they were pursued, cut down before they could even get back to the undamaged tree line. Jenks and Walsh joined the assault, helping to finish off the remnants.

"Is that all of them?" Jenks shouted. "Did we get them?"

"No," Durant said. "There's still one left."

"What?" Jenks looked around. "Where?"

"Oh no…" Durant sighed. "He's made his way over to where Clea's performing her searches. We have to get over there. Now!"

Jenks slapped Walsh's arm and gestured. "Move out! Now!"

***

Clea heard someone pound on the door, three hits high then three low. Her eyes flew over the screen, the back of her mind praying Durant built the room to withstand a beating. Text made her gasp, a single line *logs from the Tempered Steel, Zanthari An'Tufal.* "I found it! I found it!"

Her excitement was short lived. An explosion shook the room and tossed her to the floor. Smoke filled the area and her ears rang from the suddenness of it. Someone entered but she couldn't move, couldn't make her legs respond or her muscles clench. She struggled, desperate to recover any faculty, any chance to defend herself.

Her vision cleared and she saw her pistol some five feet away. Rolling on her stomach, she managed to crawl, reaching for the weapon. A blow to her side knocked the wind out of her, making her slide into the wall under the desk. She didn't have time to nurse the injury and instead pressed away, climbing to her feet unsteadily.

Another attack came, this one a punch toward her face. She faded backward, narrowly avoiding the blow. In desperation, she retaliated, throwing a feeble kick. It kept her opponent back and she pressed backward, stumbling away from the assault. A weapon cocked and she dove to the ground just as the person fired, destroying a computer console behind her.

Adrenaline cleared her head and granted her some strength. She crawled, scampering toward her gun. The enemy walked casually, rounding the table to get a clear shot at her. She rolled toward the console she'd been working at, once again taking herself out of the line of fire but away from her weapon.

Turning, Clea decided on another tactic. Moving *toward* the soldier, she climbed to her feet in a crouch and crept closer. When she saw him, he was about to turn on her. She dashed forward, grabbing his arm with the pistol and aiming it toward the ground. He peeled off several shots as she struggled to disarm him.

He punched her in the face but it wasn't enough to dislodge her. Clea smelled blood, wondered if it might be her own then saw the man's wound—the shot to the shoulder she'd scored before he scampered out. Jamming her thumb into the injury, he screamed in agony and tried to throw her off. She clung tightly to him, grinding into the hole with all her might.

A knee to her stomach made her lose some of the fight in her and he shoved her away so she collapsed on the floor. He struggled to raise his weapon, trying to point it in her direction but the offended arm would not respond. As he switched hands, Clea rushed for her gun, diving for it just as his went off.

Hot fire burned her leg as she rolled in place and unloaded her magazine. The man fired once more, a shot tapping the ground by her head even as he began to dance backwards from her attack. When he hit the ground, he heaved a gurgling sigh and went still, quite dead.

Clea didn't move for several moments, savoring the fact that she'd somehow survived unscathed. When she finally tried to stand, she realized he'd got her in the thigh just above the knee. The pain made her vision go dim and her stomach turn but she fought through it, crawling back to the terminal.

Blinking the blur from her eyes, she read the words on the screen, noting that she'd found her scan data, what they'd come all that way for. It was there, waiting to be downloaded and disseminated but just then, she couldn't make any of it out. Pain overwhelmed her and she collapsed to the floor, focusing on breathing.

Someone else came in the room, shouting her name. She recognized them as Jenks and Walsh. "I'm here…" She whispered, lifting her hand. It wasn't just the gunshot but the punch to the face, the adrenaline, the kick to her side…everything caught up to her and she didn't have it in her to move anymore. They came close and checked on her, applying pressure to the wound.

"You're going to be okay," Jenks said. "Just relax. We've got you."

"Thanks…" Clea muttered. "That was…pretty crazy."

"You sure know how to pick a mission," Walsh said. "We won, by the way."

"Never had…any doubt…" Clea smiled. "Well…just for a second."

"Be quiet. Talking's a bad idea right now." Jenks turned to Walsh. "Get one of the medics in here. We have to get her somewhere more comfortable, maybe even back to the ship. Thank God this mess is over with but holy crap what a rush."

"Is everyone else okay?" Clea asked. "Anyone else get hurt?"

Walsh cleared his throat. "Crandy's in critical condition. Jessy…well…he died. Bled out it looks like. Arak also took one to the head and Rudy's shoulder's pretty bad."

"I took a graze and you have the leg injury. All in all, considering the odds, we probably made out better than we deserved."

"Though not as we hoped…" Clea sighed. *Poor Jessy. He just wanted to leave that life behind and I suppose he has. But Arak…a solid engineer. He'll be missed. I'll have to deliver the letter to his family personally. That's not going to be an easy task.* "Be sure to let the ship know I found what we're after. This was not for nothing. I found it…"

Now I just hope it pays off. Heavens please let it pay off.

Epilogue

Gray left Adam in charge of the ship and went down to the planet personally with another contingency of marines. Not a single enemy remained alive down there, none of them surrendered and the injured ones killed themselves before they could be captured. They did manage to isolate their shuttles and confiscate their weapons though, allowing them to do *some* research on this new threat.

They landed in the clearing where the majority of the ground battle took place. He disembarked and made his way for the platform, meeting Hoffner beside a makeshift barricade. They took a tour of the battle, briefing Gray on what happened and how the men held out. Afterward, they met Durant, who was guiding robots to help clean up the mess.

"I hope you'll be coming back to the fight," Gray said to the scientist. "The alliance could definitely use everything you've got."

"If your people hadn't been here, I'd be dead now," Durant said. "They didn't hesitate to stay and protect my home. I believe I have enough of everything to help the war effort and with what Clea discovered, I'm sure we may well end this conflict soon. You have my commitment, Captain and the use of my facilities. Please contact the alliance and have them send people as soon as possible."

"You know what Clea found?" Gray asked.

Durant nodded. "Her dream turned out to be extraordinary. Who knows how long it would've been before I got to that particular record and discovered the hidden gem? A random storage drive from a forgotten battle didn't seem like a treasure but it sure has proven to be one. I'll let her explain how."

"Where is she?" Gray looked around.

"This way." Durant led the way, taking them through the foyer into a bedroom. Clea sat up on the bed, her wounded leg bandaged. She worked on a data pad, reading intently without even taking note of three people entering the room. "Um, Clea? Your captain is here to see you."

Clea looked up and her expression melted from serious to relieved. "Gray! I'm so glad to see you!"

"You too. Looks like you've had a bit of excitement." Gray approached the bed. "How're you feeling?"

"Oh, I'll be fine. The injury isn't so bad the medic said but it'll take a while to heal." Clea tapped the side of her pad. "I found it, Gray! I found it!"

"Please explain why it's so exciting," Gray replied. "What drove us through three systems to find?"

"When the attack began all those years ago, I happened to be scanning the largest ship for weaknesses, a chance to get through the shields or disable systems, anything a hack might've been for. Just before we were hit and destroyed, I uncovered something far more beneficial. As you know, the enemy ignores our hails and has not communicated with us since discovery."

"Right…" Gray nodded.

"Well, one of the reasons is their communications operate on a totally different technology than ours, much like that other species we discovered. Their codes are totally foreign to us, or so we thought. I uncovered their trick. The largest ship was broadcasting *and* decoding at the same time. I happened upon it and recorded it."

"So you can talk to the enemy now?"

"And better. Not only can we *force* communications and adapt our systems to tap into them, but they sent an FTL message back home."

Gray frowned. "Are you suggesting you know…"

Clea nodded. "Their home world. The information was lost a *long* time ago...some even said a saboteur made it happen but regardless, we haven't had coordinates for their point of origin since first contact. Now...we do."

"We'll have to verify the data," Gray said. "But otherwise, fantastic work. I'm sorry I doubted you."

"I'm sorry I gave you cause to." Clea smiled. "At least it proved to be more than a random obsession...or if it was, it paid off. Either way, discovering Durant and gaining this information will definitely make the trip worth it. The alliance is going to benefit in a major way and when we verify these coordinates, we can take the fight to them."

"Soon," Gray said. "For now, we need to keep this place safe until reinforcements arrive. These weapons can't fall into the wrong hands and now that we have them, I'm loath to leave them unguarded. Besides, you could probably use the rest planet side. Seems pretty nice out there in Durant's terraformed nature."

Clea peered out the window. "He definitely did a good job. Reminds me of the mountain you took me to on Earth."

"Good memory. Even on the verge of war, with the threat of violence, we managed to find a moment of peace." Gray leaned against the wall, peering outside. "Maybe when this is all over, we'll find it again only more permanently."

"There's always another challenge," Clea said. "Even in times without violence, we'll create obstacles to test ourselves and push our cultures to progress. I just hope they involve exploration rather than pulse cannons."

"I'll second that, Clea." Gray took a deep breath and let his shoulders relax. "Whole heartedly."

20434358R00198

Printed in Great Britain
by Amazon